# THE TWO OF US

When Mark Dexter, visiting Australia, invited Janet to work in his publishing house in the United States, she thought he was offering her heaven. They had an adventurous and thrilling trip by plane to New York, lingering in Fiji and Havana; but when they reached New York Janet found she could not get away from Julian Gaden, an odd character whom Mark had introduced her to in a Sydney night club . . .

JENNIFER AMES

# THE TWO OF US

*Complete and Unabridged*

LINFORD
*Leicester*

First published in Great Britain in 1974 by
Robert Hale Ltd
London

First Linford Edition
published 2008
by arrangement with
Robert Hale Ltd
London



British Library CIP Data

Ames, Jennifer, *1902 – 1971*
The two of us.—Large print ed.—
Linford romance library
1. Love stories 2. Large type books
I. Title
823.9′14 [F]

ISBN 978–1–84782–260–4

Published by
F. A. Thorpe (Publishing)
Anstey, Leicestershire

Set by Words & Graphics Ltd.
Anstey, Leicestershire
Printed and bound in Great Britain by
T. J. International Ltd., Padstow, Cornwall

This book is printed on acid-free paper

# 1

'Have you ever thought of going over and visiting the United States, Janet?' Mark Dexter asked.

It might have been just a casual remark over the luncheon table. But there had been a strangely intent note in his voice as though he intended her to take it seriously. They were seated over the luncheon table at Jones' Restaurant, looking down on to Whale Beach. The views were magnificent and it had been a very good lunch.

'I've often thought of going to the United States,' she said slowly. 'Especially as . . . ' She broke off, but her pretty face was flushed and her bright hazel eyes were eager.

'Especially as — ' he caught her up 'Don't go on if you don't want to,' he said. 'But I hate unfinished sentences.'

She hesitated. 'I have a sister over

there,' she told him finally. But she looked away from him as she said it, biting her lip, hating to have to tell the lie — that stupid lie. What else could she do in the circumstances?

'That would make your visit all the pleasanter.'

'But I couldn't visit, I should have to work,' she told him bluntly. 'And since as an Australian I can't come in on the quota — it's closed for about thirty years — I could only go as a visitor and I haven't the money for that.'

'But you want to go?' he insisted again, leaning further over the table.

'Oh, yes! It's been a dream of mine for years.' She hesitated again, and murmured, 'Ever since Daddy died.'

'We might arrange the financial side of it,' Mark Dexter said crisply. 'You could work for our company, the East-West Publishing Company. You could read manuscripts and advise. It needn't be a regular job, so you wouldn't come up against the migration restrictions.'

'You really think I might do that?' Her eyes were suddenly full of tears and she was ashamed of them.

He saw the tears. He patted one of her hands on the table. 'You really want to go as much as that? Well then, of course, it must be arranged. But what will your boss, Alvin Harvey, have to say to me if I take you away from the Hamilton Publishing Company over here? He's been pretty decent to me ever since I've come out to Australia looking for new manuscripts. I shouldn't like to take you away from him if you feel you're absolutely necessary in his office here.'

'I was going to resign anyhow,' Janet said.

'You were? I thought you were highly thought of in the firm. I thought you liked your work.'

'Oh, I do,' she told him. 'It's just — well — ' she hesitated and shrugged — 'one of those things. As I said, I had intended to resign.'

He didn't ask the reason for her

intended resignation and she was grateful. But her boss, Alvin Harvey, a big powerful man in his middle forties, had come to like her too much of late. He was always asking her for dinner dates, offering to drive her home. He had a wife and family, and Janet was very much attached to Edith Harvey. She certainly didn't want to figure as the other woman in the case, especially as she didn't love him. She had been on the point of handing in her resignation when Alvin Harvey had suddenly said to her, 'I've a special assignment for you during the next week or so, Janet. A good friend of mine from the States, Mark Dexter, managing director of the East-West Publishing Company, will be in Sydney for a short time, trying to pick up some manuscripts he would like to publish in the States. He doesn't know his way around and asked me if I could find someone to act as a guide for him. I thought of you, Janet. Would you care for the assignment? It would be in the nature of a holiday for you.'

She had agreed, though she had no idea what this Mark Dexter would be like. She was surprised and pleased the first day Alvin Harvey introduced her to him in the office. He was well over six foot tall, with a slim athletic build, pleasantly handsome features, with a cleft in his chin and nice steel-grey eyes. His smile was warm and charming.

He held out his hand to her. 'So you're to be my guide round Sydney during the next few days, Miss Freeman. I'm in luck. I couldn't have wished for a nicer-looking guide. I hope you will take me to all the exciting places. By the way, I've hired a car for the period I shall be in Sydney. There are so many things I want to see in this vast new country — the harbour and coastline, the Blue Mountains, as well as all the Australian publishers. You'll be kept pretty busy.' Again he gave her that warm charming smile.

'I'll be glad to be of any service I can be,' Janet replied demurely.

She felt gay and light-hearted at the

prospect of showing this delightful young American around Sydney. He couldn't have been more than twenty-eight or -nine.

Alvin Harvey frowned slightly as though the first interview between them had gone a little too well for his liking. But he happened to be up to his eyes in work. He would entertain Mark at his house, of course, but he hadn't any time during the day to spare for taking him about. But he wondered if he had made a wise decision. He didn't want any man taking Janet from him. As yet there had been nothing except friendship between them, but he was very hopeful. Young girls often fell in love with middle-aged men, he argued to himself. They hadn't youth to give them, but they had wisdom, experience and sophistication.

The days had gone quickly — almost too quickly for Janet. Mark was entertaining, companionable, and she liked the flurry his good looks caused amongst the women in the restaurants he took her to. He never seemed to care about expense. They lunched at Princes, the Australia, the Caprice, Romano's, and all the smartest places. They visited other publishers and picked up manuscripts. Mark had told Janet exactly what he wanted and she would look the manuscripts through for him at night and decide whether or not he would be interested in taking them back to the States with him.

'You're quite an invaluable help to me,' he told her several times, earnestly and seriously.

That was another thing she liked about him. He would be laughing one moment and the next he would be completely serious. He was serious now about this trip of hers to the U.S.A., and her heart missed a beat.

It was no longer only the prospect of going to the States which left her almost dumbfounded with excitement; it would mean she would be constantly seeing Mark in his office. Maybe out of office hours as well; he had told her he was a bachelor. She had had love affairs in the past, rather mild ones. She had never found herself attracted to any man as she was to Mark Dexter. She liked everything about him, and the more she saw of him the more she liked him. It would be easy, fatally easy, to fall in love with him.

But as yet he had made no sign that he was attracted towards her; he hadn't even asked her to kiss him. But he had suggested she come to the U.S. The thought excited her so that her heart pounded rapidly and little veins throbbed in her temples.

'It would be quite easy to get you a visitor's permit for six months,' he told her. 'And after that you've only got to go out of the country for a few days and then you can re-enter. You could go to Mexico. Have you ever been to Acapulco in Mexico? It's a wonderful place. To my mind it has more charm than any beauty spot on the Riviera. We could easily spend a few days there and then you would be quite entitled to re-enter the United States for another six months.'

'It sounds like heaven,' she said, breathing rapidly.

He smiled. 'Then that's more or less settled. You'd better talk to Alvin Harvey tonight and then we could go round to the American Consulate and make arrangements. You say you have a sister living in America; that will help.'

She liked him so much she would have liked to tell him the truth. It was too stupid to have to lie about the relationship between her mother and herself. But her mother had insisted that if she ever came over to the States she must act as her sister. 'No one must ever know I was married before I married Tim Warren,' her mother had written shortly after her father's death. Until her father's death they hadn't corresponded for years. 'Besides, Tim is so much younger than I am. I would be embarrassed to have to present you as my daughter. I know the whole situation may seem strange to you, dearest, but believe me, as far as I'm concerned it's for the best. I couldn't have it any other way. Tim will know, of course, but he's the only one who will know.'

It was strange to think about her mother. She had been dead to her for so many years, ever since she had deserted her father and herself and left for America with Tim Warren, a much younger man. She had been very bitter about the desertion all through her childhood, and she knew her father had suffered very deeply. When her father had asked her not to correspond with her mother during his lifetime she had agreed. It was only ten years later, after her father's death, that she had received the first letter from her mother. It was curiously signed, 'Your sister, June Warren.'

At first she had been very bitter about it, deeply resenting the fact that her mother refused to acknowledge her as her daughter, but with the passing years she had more or less got used to the strange situation. If her mother insisted upon it, why should she care? But it was queer to have a mother who claimed to be her elder sister. What would happen when they met?

She had loved her mother very dearly as a child. The shock of her departure when she had come back to the house after school one day and found all her mother's clothes gone from the closet, her drawers empty, had aged her years. Her father had been heartbroken. He divorced her mother, but he remained heartbroken until he died. She felt she could never forgive her mother that. And yet the urge to see her again was wellnigh irresistible. Even though you disapproved of what your mother had done, even though at one time you had hated her, the tie of blood was very strong. And now in her early twenties, with a B.A. at Sydney University behind her, Janet told herself she felt differently about the whole situation. If she ever went to the States, she would meet her mother on her mother's ground — her younger sister. But until today she had never thought that the prospect of going to the States and meeting her mother after this long lapse of years was at all possible.

'In the past few days I've come to rely upon you in an almost unbelievable manner,' Mark was saying. 'You know just the sort of books I want. I scarcely need to read them through. You would be invaluable to me in the States. Think it over, Janet, please. Of course I'll pay your fare there and back.'

'I have no need to think it over,' Janet said with a half-scared, half-excited laugh. 'I've quite decided to come, if you will have me. I'll tell my boss in the morning about it.'

Mark grimaced. 'He won't be very pleased with me — loaning you to me in the first place and then having me pinch you from him.'

'I'll tell him I was going to resign anyhow,' she said. 'I hope I'll make him understand.'

'Alvin Harvey has always been a very

good friend to me. I shouldn't like to break the friendship,' Mark remarked. 'But' — his voice lowered — 'I want you to come with me, Janet. It's years since I've wished for anything so much.'

The colour stained her cheeks, her heart beat rapidly again.

'As you know, I have to go to Victoria, South Australia and Western Australia for several weeks. Could you be ready to fly back with me say in three weeks' time?'

Could she be ready! She could be ready this minute. She had never felt so excited about anything in the whole of her life. To see America, to work with Mark, to live in New York City — all unbelievable a few days ago. And now she was being offered all these chances on a silver platter. She would see her mother again, of course, though her feelings were very mixed concerning her. She had gone through deep grief, a period of hatred, and now something strangely approaching indifference. Yet for all that, she was full of curiosity.

‘I’d like to seal our bargain with a kiss,’ Mark said, smiling. ‘But this is rather a public place. Do you know you’re a very pretty girl, Janet?’

‘I’m glad you like my looks,’ she said, and she meant that sincerely. She was more than glad — she was thrilled. It was the first direct compliment he had paid her.

‘I’m dining with Alvin and his wife tonight,’ he said. ‘If you like, I’ll break the news to him. I’ll ask him if I can borrow you for the next six months. That may make it easier. After that, if you like it over there, you can stay on.’

‘Oh, I’ll like it,’ she said. ‘It’s the most wonderful chance I’ve ever had in my life.’

He caught both her hands under the table. ‘You’ve been very sweet to me, Janet, very patient. Besides, you’ve done one heck of a lot of work for me, saved me endless hours of reading. I should like to make it up to you. I think perhaps I can make it up to you.’

She let him hold her hands under the table, squeezing them tightly. It sent a shock of emotion through her. She had thought herself in love in her teens, but it was nothing compared with this. To be loved, to be going to travel halfway round the world with the man she loved; to be going to work for him once she arrived in the States.

I'm keeping my fingers crossed, she thought. Oh dear, I hope nothing happens to prevent this. I hope Alvin Harvey doesn't cut up rough.

After luncheon they took a stroll along the cliffs. Suddenly he caught her by the shoulders, and turned her round to face him.

'I feel if I kiss you it will bring us both luck,' he said.

He drew her closer and she raised her trembling lips to his. 'Luck to both of us,' he said, 'and a happy new relationship, Janet. You're a really wonderful girl.'

She said, 'Thank you,' in a muffled voice and kissed him back and then they proceeded arm in arm along the cliff path.

It was a wonderful day. She didn't know when a day had been more wonderful in her whole life.

# 2

It had been an inspired moment that moment on the cliffside, and later he hadn't presumed upon it. As he had told her, he was going to dinner with the Harveys. She went back to the house in Glebe which she shared with three other girls.

'You look very pleased with yourself,' one of them, Mavis, said to her.

She laughed and clasped her hands above her head. 'I'm besotted with happiness. I've just been offered a trip to the United States.'

'You have!' Mavis, rather a plain girl with spectacles, stared at her, almost speechless. 'Who's sending you? Your boss?'

She shook her head. 'No. I'm going in connection with an American publishing firm, The East-West Publishing Company.'

'You think you'll get a visa?' Mavis asked.

She nodded. 'I think I'll get a visitor's visa anyhow. After that, I believe it's quite in order to go out of the States for a short while and then re-enter.'

'You're the lucky one,' Mavis said. 'Here am I in the drudgery of teaching stupid giggling brats — not one of them knows or cares what you're talking about. But what will your boss at the Hamilton Publishing Company have to say?'

'I'd already written out my resignation about ten days ago. I didn't deliver it because this new job cropped up. But I'll give it to Mr. Harvey tomorrow.'

'He won't like that,' Mavis said. 'He's always driving you home of an evening, and more than once you've dined with him, haven't you?'

'But only to talk business,' Janet said quickly. 'He's married and has a family of four children.'

'Well then perhaps it's just as well you're going,' Mavis said. 'You don't want to be involved in a scandal at your age.'

'I certainly do not,' Janet said positively. 'Besides, I like his wife Edith very much.'

She went up to her room and looked over her wardrobe. It would have to do. She would rather spend what money she had saved on new clothes in the States. She had heard they were smarter and cheaper in America.

She looked down at her desk and saw the last letter she had received from her mother fully three months ago. Her mother had never made any suggestion she should visit her. Would she be pleased or annoyed that Janet was coming? Would she look too young to be a sister — even a much younger sister? Her mother must be forty-two, some difference in age from Janet's twenty-two. Was that why her mother hadn't ever asked her over? Or had she in the passing years become more or less indifferent to her as Janet had become to her? Yet surely she was curious to see this daughter whom she had abandoned as a child? Janet assured herself that her main feeling about seeing her mother was curiosity. She had forgiven her all these long years of loneliness in her childhood when she had been at boarding school and other girls' mothers had come of a Wednesday afternoon and she had had no one to visit her. Her father, a professor, was too occupied to come down on visiting days.

She wasn't looking forward to the following morning. She didn't quite know how her boss would take her resignation. She would tell him that she had decided to resign some time ago. But would he believe her? She would give him the letter she had written some weeks previously. She hoped Mark had paved the way for her successfully.

But the next morning when she arrived at the office, Alvin Harvey looked black as thunder.

'What's this I hear about you going

off to America with Mark Dexter?' he shot at her once they were alone in the office.

'He has offered me the trip. It seems too good an opportunity to pass up. For several reasons I've always wanted to visit the States.'

'What about your job with me? Does that mean nothing to you?' he thundered at her.

'It's meant a great deal in the past, Mr. Harvey,' she said quietly. 'But as a matter of fact, I was going to resign before I met Mr. Dexter. I have the letter here. You will see by the date it was written over two weeks ago.'

He looked dumbfounded. 'Why the devil should you want to resign? I rely upon you for so many things, Janet. In fact' — he lowered his voice — 'I'm very much attached to you.'

She nodded slowly. 'I know that, Mr. Harvey. I think that's one reason I'd better leave the firm. I am very fond of your wife. She has been a very good friend to me in the past.'

'But Edith isn't jealous of my relationship with you, Janet!' Alvin cried. 'We've never given her any cause to be jealous.'

'Not yet,' she said, keeping her voice low. 'But it might happen, Mr. Harvey. I've thought for some time it may be better if I made a change.'

'Better for whom — for you or me?' he asked her bluntly.

'A little time ago you were suggesting you took a flat for me, so that I could live on my own. You also suggested a trip to Surfers' Paradise.'

'Damn it all! Am I so repulsive to you?' he cried out in a rage.

She shook her head. 'No, not repulsive, Mr. Harvey. But I don't mix business with pleasure — at least not with that sort of pleasure. Please understand what I mean. I'm truly sorry that it happened.'

He slumped back in his chair. The big broad-shouldered man seemed deflated.

'I wouldn't have made any demands

on you other than you wished, Janet,' he said finally.

'But I couldn't accept all that from you and not give in to any demands you might wish to make,' she pointed out. 'I've enjoyed working here. I'm grateful to you and your wife for your friendship to me. It was through you two that I've got this magnificent chance of going to the United States.'

'I never would have suggested that you look after Mark Dexter if I'd thought this was going to happen,' he mumbled. 'How is he so different from me?'

'Ours will be purely a business relationship. He's made that quite clear. Besides, he's a bachelor. There's no wife to be hurt if I do stay back working late with him or accept an occasional invitation to dinner.'

'And he's much younger,' Alvin Harvey growled.

'Yes, he's much younger,' Janet said, and added, 'I've never wanted to be an older man's plaything, Mr. Harvey.'

‘Get out!’ he said, raising his voice. ‘You can leave tomorrow, if you like.’

‘I should like it very much,’ Janet retorted. ‘And I don’t want any salary for the past two weeks. It’s been all a pleasure. But I do thank you, Mr Harvey, for everything you’ve done for me. Don’t think I’m not grateful for that, at least.’

He merely grunted and turned to a pile of correspondence which he flicked over without seeing what was written on the pages. His heart was sore inside him; he was bitter with disappointment. He knew he wanted Janet Freeman; he might even be in love with her.

* * *

Janet already had a passport. A year before she had planned a trip with some other girls to Hong Kong. The trip had fallen through at the last moment: one of the girls had become ill, and besides, Mr. Harvey had said he couldn’t spare her at that special juncture, so the trip had been indefinitely postponed. But the passport was good.

Mark took her down to the American Consulate that afternoon. She was finger-printed and all the necessary arrangements were made. It was almost too easy. She had a six-months visitor's visa, which they told her could be extended. The immigration regulations were not as strict as they used to be. She felt hazy with delirious excitement. She even wrote down that her nearest relative in New York was her sister, Mrs. June Warren, without feeling any unnecessary sense of guilt.

She considered cabling her mother, but decided in the end not to write; she would surprise her. Her curiosity about her mother had given way to an intense sense of excitement. She wanted more than anything in this world to walk across her mother's threshold and say, 'Here am I, Janet. Am I anything like the child you left behind in Australia ten years ago?'

In the excitement of her thought of their reunion, she had forgiven her mother all that she had made her and her father suffer when she had eloped with handsome, debonair Tim Warren. Tim was an American. She could remember him as being distinctly handsome, blond, blue-eyed. She herself had had a girlish crush on him. He crooned at the piano and her mother accompanied him. But apart from that she had no notion what he did. She knew they had a flat on Washington Square — a penthouse flat, her mother had described it in a letter. So they must be wealthy. But still she had extended no invitation to Janet to come and visit her. She told her that she also ran a beauty salon in the East Fifties. 'Very exclusive,' she had written. 'Most of the New York prominent society women are our clients.' Did Tim manage the beauty salon? What was his work? Her mother had never mentioned him in connection with any other job. She had mentioned a Monsieur

Charles, who she said was a wizard at doing women's hair.

Dexter smiled at her and said, 'Are you pleased?' as they left the Consulate with everything arranged.

She laughed back at him. 'I'm so dizzy, I feel as though I'm walking on my head.'

'Let's go into the Australia lounge to have a cocktail to celebrate,' he said quickly. 'But don't walk there on your head, please.'

As they sat down at a table in the first-floor lounge he asked, 'When you first arrive in New York, will you be staying with your sister?'

She was hesitant. 'I don't know, I don't know if she has the room for me. I rather think she can't have, or else she would have invited me over before.'

'Well I can easily fix that up,' Mark said. 'Most of the better hotels have very nice one-room apartments. I'll book you in at the Beekman Towers Hotel. It's just round by the United Nations, and you get a lovely view up the East River from the top apartments.'

She looked alarmed. 'It sounds luxurious. Will I be able to afford it?'

'Don't worry — you will,' he said. 'You've rendered me excellent service so far. I'm going to see that the firm makes good use of you and you'll be paid well for it, Janet.'

'I don't know how to thank you,' she stammered. 'You've only been ten days in my life and yet everything's been changed.'

He took her hand and drew her towards him. They were sitting on a settee in a far corner of the room. 'I want to be a lot more than ten days in your life, Janet Freeman. Why else do you think I've bothered about making all these arrangements about your coming to the States?'

Her heart turned over. It was all too good, too thrilling, too exciting.

'Did Alvin Harvey mind very much?' he asked. 'When I mentioned the subject to him last night he shut up like a clam. He wasn't so awfully friendly to me for the rest of the evening.'

'He didn't like it,' she agreed. 'But when I told him I would have been leaving anyhow, he seemed more or less resigned.'

'He's a queer fellow,' Mark said. 'Always has been as long as I've known him. He has everything to make him happy — a prosperous business, a charming wife and family — and yet I have the feeling he's always yearning for something.' He looked at her slyly and added, 'It couldn't be you he's yearning after, Janet?'

She felt that the hot flush that rushed into her cheeks had given her away.

'Come on, admit it if it's true,' he teased her softly.

'I don't like to admit it,' she said. 'But I do think he had a yen for me. That's why I wrote out my resignation. But I don't think it's really over me — I think he has a longing for his past youth. He likes to think he's fifteen years younger than he is. He plays squash and skin-dives with much younger men and women. He won't accept the fact he's getting older.'

'Too bad,' Mark said. 'But it's as well you'll be free of him, Janet. Edith Harvey is a charming woman; I wouldn't want to see that marriage broken up.'

'Nor I,' said Janet, fervently. 'That's one reason your offer to come to America was heaven-sent.'

'Shall we dine somewhere tonight and dance at Chequers?' he suggested. 'You know I'm leaving for Melbourne in the morning, and when I come back we'll have less than a day before we board the plane.'

Chequers was always gay and amusing. The food was good, the floor show of international and Australian artistes excellent.

They had finished the first dance and were returning to their table, where a champagne bottle stood in its ice-bucket waiting for them, when suddenly a man clapped Mark on the shoulder.

'Well, of all that's wonderful! Mark Dexter!'

The stranger was a tall, loose-jointed man, but he gave the impression of quick action and hard muscles. He had very dark hair, which flopped loosely and untidily down on to his forehead. His eyes were blue, intensely blue.

'Julian Gaden!' Mark exclaimed. 'Fancy running into you down here! I'd no idea you'd come Down Under.'

'I came on a little job,' said the other man. 'But it's finished. I'm all alone here tonight. Mind if I join up with you?'

'We should be delighted,' said Mark. 'Let me introduce Miss Janet Freeman.'

'You've certainly picked yourself a pretty girl since you've been in Sydney,' said Julian, winking at Mark. 'I'm afraid I've had no such luck. The dames I've been mixing up with are of a tougher variety. I'll hop back to my table pay my bill, and join you in a few minutes.' He added tentatively, 'I say, I hope I'm not butting in?'

'Not at all,' Mark said politely and insincerely.

As they approached their table, Mark said to Janet, 'I hope you didn't mind my including Julian Gaden in the party?'

'No, not since he's a friend of yours,' Janet said. But she did mind — terribly. This was to be her last night out with Mark for some time. She wanted to be alone with him. She had wanted very much to be alone with him ever since that time on the cliff-path between Palm and Whale Beach when he had taken her in his arms and kissed her. She hadn't forgotten one single moment of that experience. She wanted to feel the pressure of his lips again — longed to feel them. Had it just been a casual kiss or had he meant something more? Would she know in the future? Would she have to wait until they got to the United States to find out?

'I shouldn't say he was a particular friend of mine,' Mark said. 'He's an odd fellow, Julian Gaden. Lord alone knows what he does for a living, but when any trouble starts, he always seems to be there. I suppose he has private means — I know he has no special job. I always looked upon him as a typical New Yorker. I should have said he'd hate to leave it, even for a single moment. Queer to find him out here. Very queer.'

What he had told her didn't make Janet feel any more kindly disposed towards Julian Gaden.

Her silence obviously made him uneasy.

'You didn't mind my asking him to join us?' he asked anxiously. 'But damn it all, what else could I do?'

'No, I don't see what else you could have done,' she agreed, 'other than being rude to him.'

'If this had been our last evening alone, Janet, I would have risked being rude to him. But after all, I'll be back in three weeks' time and then we'll be starting on our flight to the U.S. We'll have plenty more evenings together, plenty more opportunities to talk.'

Presently Julian Gaden joined their table. In the soft light of the table lamp he was considerably better looking than she had at first supposed him to be. He had a long well-shaped nose, a hard jaw and high cheekbones. He had a high forehead, over which the dark black hair loosely flopped. Every now and then he raised a hand and pushed it back almost savagely.

'You haven't told me yet what brings you out here, Julian,' Mark reminded him.

Julian grinned. He had a most infectious grin that lit up his whole face and made it more than ever attractive. 'I've been playing chaperone to a rock-'n'-roll singer. She was some baby. She wanted to keep the public at arm's length and keep the jewels she'd brought along with her for herself. Gaby Holaway; she was on at the stadium in Sydney. Have you by any chance seen her?'

Mark shook his head and smiled. 'I'm afraid rock-'n'-roll singers are not much in my line.'

'She was a big hit out here. It took me all my time getting her some privacy. But she's flown back to the States today. I thought I'd stay on and look around a while. This sure is an attractive country. When are you going back Mark?'

'In three weeks' time, by Quantas Airways. Janet Freeman is coming along with me. She's going to do some work for my firm in New York.'

Julian grinned again, as though he half believed the story — the worse half, that was. He was staring so hard at Janet it made her uncomfortable.

'Do you know, you remind me of someone,' he said finally. 'You're younger, of course, but you have her way of walking and certain of her mannerisms. You don't happen to have any relatives in New York?'

'My sister lives in Washington Square,' she told him. 'Her name is

Mrs. Tim Warren.'

She saw him start. A look almost of unbelief passed across his features for a moment. 'Did you say Tim Warren's wife June is your sister?' he demanded. His voice was harsh, urgent.

'Yes, June Warren is my sister.' But how Janet hated to lie, even to this man whom she scarcely knew.

'The Madame June who runs a big beauty salon in the Fifties?' Julian demanded.

Janet nodded. 'Yes, I believe she does.'

'I must say you look a lot younger than your sister,' he commented. 'Though she's smart and good looking enough.'

Now Janet had started on the lie, she had to carry on. 'There is a big difference in our ages.'

Julian chuckled. 'I take it you were an afterthought. No one more surprised than Pa and Ma when you came along. Do you know her husband Tim?'

'I met him years ago,' Janet said. 'I

doubt if I'd recognise him if I saw him again.'

'He's quite a guy,' Julian said. 'He must be in his middle thirties, but he seems younger, as handsome as they come.'

Janet was curious.

'What does he do? Does he help my sister in the beauty salon?'

'He has his way of making money — that's for sure,' Julian said. 'But if you ask me what exactly he does do, I couldn't tell you. There are lots of fellows around New York like him, always busy, always up to something or other. But if you tried to pin them down to exactly what they're working on, there's nothing doing.'

Mark laughed. 'That rather goes for you, Julian. I don't know what the heck you do except you've just told me you've played the big chaperone to a rock'n'roll singer. That certainly surprises me. I didn't think anything would pry you out of little old New York.'

'Gaby Holaway happens to be a friend,' he said. 'I wanted to see all went well with her.'

'I never knew a man with so many friends,' Mark went on. 'You have them in every class of society.'

Julian grinned again. 'I admit I'm sociable. Is there any harm in that?'

'I don't suppose so, so long as the cash comes rolling in.'

'I'm all right financially,' Julian said, and grinned again. 'Were you worried I'd make a touch, Mark? Now supposing I dance with this charming lady, Miss Janet Freeman? Have you any objections, Mark?'

'Go ahead and dance,' Mark said.

He danced well in a loose-jointed way. He was always inventing intricate steps, which Janet found it hard to follow. She preferred dancing with Mark. His was a smoother, more conventional style. She couldn't quite describe her feelings towards Julian Gaden. He was vivacious, amusing, the height of friendliness, but she had a strange feeling it was all a cover. A cover for what? What was the real Julian Gaden like inside that cover of exuberant good humour? His face, though attractive, was tough looking. She could feel the hard ripple of his muscles as they danced. She felt he would be a good person to have beside you in a tight spot. But why should she ever be in a tight spot and need the protection of someone like Julian Gaden? It was an odd thought and she dismissed it.

'I gather Mark is going to Western Australia for the next few weeks,' Julian said. 'Would you dine with me some night — and make it soon? I may not be around here long. At any moment I may be flying back. I'd like to talk to you about Tim Warren and your sister.'

Was the mention of Tim Warren and her mother merely a bait? She didn't know whether she wanted to dine with him, but there could be no harm and she was definitely curious. She knew so little of her mother and her life in New

York, so little of the handsome young American she had eloped with.

'Very well. I'd be pleased to dine with you, Mr. Gaden.'

'Call me Julian. Since you're June's sister, we're bound to be seeing a great deal of each other in New York. May I call you by your first name? I think Mark introduced you as Miss Janet Freeman. Janet. That's a mighty pretty name.'

'Thank you,' she said.

The dance was ended and they went back to their table.

'I've asked this girl to dine with me one night early next week,' Julian said to Mark. 'Any objections?'

Mark said a little stiffly, 'It's entirely up to Janet.'

'She's agreed,' Julian said, and grinned.

'Then there was scarcely any need to ask my approval.' Mark's voice was still distinctly cool.

Julian winked across to Janet. 'I seem to be treading on Mark's toes. All the same, I'm going to hold you to that dinner date. What's today — Friday? Let's make it Monday. I may be gone shortly after that. Give me your address and I'll pick you up. I'll leave a choice of the restaurant to you. I've learned quite a bit about Sydney following Gaby Holaway about, but maybe you have some special favourite restaurant.'

'I like Princes as well as any place,' Janet said. 'I like its old-fashioned atmosphere.'

'Princes it shall be, and I'll pick you up around six-thirty.'

Shortly after that he said he would be moving on and left them. Janet was glad to see him go. She still wasn't at all sure whether or not she liked him.

'What did you think of Julian? Mark wanted to know.

Janet took a little time in replying. 'I really don't know. He's pleasant and sociable enough, but at the same time he's aggressive and determined.'

'Julian is all that,' Mark agreed. 'But

you seem to have made a hit with him. I'm not sure I altogether like this dinner date on Monday night.'

'He said he wanted to talk to me about my sister and Tim Warren.'

'But that may only be an excuse,' Mark objected. 'You're a dashed pretty girl, Janet. So fresh and unaffected, too. You'll have half the men in New York going nuts about you.'

She smiled across at him. 'You American men are immensely flattering. I don't believe you mean half of it.'

'Just wait and see,' he promised. 'You'll be a sensation, Janet.'

They stayed on talking and dancing until the final cabaret was over. He drove her home to the house in Glebe she shared with the other three girls.

'May I kiss you, Janet?' he asked softly and with humility. 'It's by way of thanking you. I've had such a wonderful ten days with you.'

'If you wish, Mark.' She raised her lips. They trembled under his. She felt her whole being responding to his kiss.

'It's been a wonderful ten days for me,' she whispered.

'Bless you. I'll enjoy having you in New York, Janet. Apart from the help you'll be able to give me with those Australian manuscripts, I feel we're really friends.'

But although her whole being ached for it, he had said no word of love. And she wouldn't see him for three whole weeks. She was a little downcast as she made her way up the flight of stairs towards her small attic bedroom.

# 3

Janet went into the office on the Monday to start clearing out her desk and giving the girl who would follow her, a Miss Hertzog, full instructions. Alvin Harvey spoke to her brusquely and it hurt her more than a little that they couldn't part as friends. But apparently he had resented very much what she had said to him the other day.

That evening promptly at six-thirty Julian Gaden called to take her out to dinner. She showed him into their sitting-room on the ground floor. It was an attractive room, old-fashioned high ceilings, furnished in antique pieces the girls had picked up on countless rambles through old furniture shops.

'Very nice here,' he remarked. 'I hope you don't think I'm rushing you, Janet, but to tell you the truth, I never know where I'll be from one day to the next.'

'That's all right,' she said, and smiled at him. 'I have nothing else to do this evening.'

'Hey, that's not much of a compliment to me,' he said and grinned. He had a nice infectious grin that made his long lean strong-featured face almost handsome.

She had placed a decanter of sherry and two glasses on the table. She invited him to have one with her.

'Sherry,' he commented. 'That has an old-fashioned flavour like the rest of this room. We Americans don't go much on sherry. We go more for hard liquor in the States.'

'I'm sorry, I have nothing else to offer you.'

He laughed. 'Don't take it like that. I'm not always over-careful in what I say. I'd be proud to have a glass of sherry with you, Janet, and then we'll be moving on. I've booked a table at that restaurant you mentioned — Princes. I hope we get to dance there.'

'Yes, there's an orchestra.'

Two of the other girls, Judy and Mavis, came in while they were drinking their sherry. They joined them in a glass and for a while the conversation was general.

'You certainly go in for Yanks,' Mavis said in an undertone to Janet while they were taking some glasses out into the kitchen. 'How come? This is the second one you've had in tow in the past two weeks.'

'I met him the other night when I was out with Mark,' she said. 'He invited me to dinner.'

'Good on you, girl.' Mavis nodded approvingly. 'The Yanks know how to spend money. That's one thing for sure.'

She said she didn't want a cocktail when they arrived at Princes, so they went straight to their dinner table. It was a nice table, poised on a tier above the dance-floor. The whole atmosphere of the restaurant had grace and ease and luxury.

'You go for old-fashioned places, don't you, Janet?' Julian commented. 'We have old Colonial places in New York. They're quite the rage. Connecticut and Long Island are full of antique shops. Almost every second house you pass on the highroad is an antique shop, selling old Colonial furniture — most of it fake.' His eyes narrowed and he asked, 'Are you going to live in New York with your sister?'

'I don't think so,' she said. 'I'd rather be independent. Mark spoke of taking an apartment for me in Beekman Towers Hotel.'

'That's a fine hotel,' he commented. 'But how come you're not going to stay with your sister?'

'Their apartment might not be big enough.'

'Not big enough!' He threw back his head and laughed. 'Ye gods, it's a penthouse apartment, but inside it's a palace. It's one of New York's show places. June and Tim entertain a lot.'

Yet she's never asked me over to visit

her, Janet thought, and the knowledge hurt.

'How long is it since you've seen your sister?' Julian went on.

'Ten — almost eleven years,' Janet answered.

He pursed his lips into a whistle. 'Eleven years? That's a good long stretch of time. You must have been just a kid when she left home.'

'I was,' Janet replied.

'Eleven years is a long stretch of a person's life. She wasn't Madame June then, was she, of the Madame June Beauty Salon in East Fifty-fifth Street? Both Tim and she have come a long way in the past years.'

'What does he do?' Janet asked because she was frankly curious.

He shrugged. 'Blessed if I know. Maybe he operates on the stock exchange; maybe he plays the gee-gees. He always seems to have plenty of ready cash on hand. They live a fast-moving life over there, Janet. Quite different from the life you lead over here. Do you think you're wise to try it? Aren't you satisfied where you are? If I were you' — and he spoke the next words slowly — 'I'd think more than once — or even more than twice — before I set off on this proposed journey to the United States.' He had been laughing a moment before, but now his voice was very grave. It seemed as though he were warning her. 'Yes,' he repeated, 'I'd think very seriously before deciding on this trip, Janet.'

She stared across at him in astonishment. For a moment he had seemed a different person from the free and easy, rather aggressive young American she had taken him to be at first. He seemed older, wiser, and very intent upon what he said. She stared across at him in frank astonishment. 'You're not suggesting I should give up the prospect of this marvellous trip to the United States?'

'I am,' he said in that same grave serious voice. 'You don't know what you will be stepping into, Janet. There may be unpleasantness; there may even be danger.'

'Danger?' She caught up the word sharply. Her voice was shocked, incredulous. 'But how can it possibly be dangerous? I'm going to work for the East-West Publishing Company. They've promised me a handsome salary — much more than I earn over here.'

'Mark Dexter is a generous employer. He seems to have been especially generous in your case.' His voice was slightly dry. 'But when I mentioned danger, I was referring more to your social life than your business activities. A young girl, if I may say so, as pretty as you are, in New York needs a fairly level head or else she is liable to go right under.'

'I think I have a fairly level head,' she said shortly. She felt angry with him, furious really. He was trying to spoil the pleasure of this intended trip, all the excitement it offered her.

He chuckled grimly. 'You're mad at

me, aren't you? You're living in a dream-world, Janet. Wonderful things seem waiting for you just around the corner. But what if you don't like your sister's set of friends? Whom would you have to turn to?'

'I'd have Mark, of course.'

'Yes, and come right slap bang up against Coleen Hausman.'

'What do you mean?' Her voice sounded slightly rattled suddenly. 'And who is Coleen Hausman?'

He raised one dark untidy eyebrow. 'Mark hasn't told you about her?'

She shook her head. 'It's the first time I've heard her name mentioned.'

'She's by way of being a friend of his — a very great friend, so rumour has it. They've known each other most of their lives. She was Coleen Cameron and then she married Henry Hausman. But the marriage didn't last long. He died.' Momentarily his voice hardened. 'Mark's and Coleen's names are always being coupled together in the gossip columns. Coleen is the daughter — the only child — of

Colonel John Cameron, a millionaire on the stock exchange. It's odd Mark hasn't mentioned her name to you.'

Her heart turned over with a sudden fear, but she managed to make her voice casual as she said, 'After all, Mark and I have only known each other ten days. We haven't had time to talk of all his friends.'

'Have you talked of any of his friends?' he asked her sharply.

Again she felt annoyance and resentment, and that odd sense of fear.

'It's difficult to talk of people you don't know. I know that his mother and father live in Ridgefield, Connecticut. There is a sister Anne, who has recently married a young doctor.'

'Mark plays in high society,' Julian said. 'He's a prominent member of the social set in New York. They call it Café Society. I doubt if you'd feel at home with them.'

'Do you mean you don't think I'd fit in?'

'They're a closed-in set. They don't

welcome newcomers.'

She was furious with him once again. 'Are you trying to tell me I wouldn't be welcomed in Mark's New York set?'

'Frankly, I don't know,' he said. 'But I don't think Coleen Hausman is a girl who would welcome a potential rival. And she's one of the leaders of the set, pretty, sophisticated, the only daughter of a millionaire.'

'Are you trying to insinuate I have nothing to offer in place of that?' she cried indignantly.

'You have a very pretty face and a lovely figure. So has Coleen, and she will one day inherit millions as well. That's why I'm wondering — it's just an idea, mind you — if you wouldn't be happier staying here where you belong, in Sydney.'

But she was still too furious with him to think the matter over reasonably.

'Why are you trying to put me off going to New York?' she asked. 'What has it do with you? First you suggest I may not be happy in my sister's set;

then you suggest I might be equally unhappy in the New York society in which Mark mixes. But I'm not planning to go to New York for a social life; I'm planning to go there to broaden my experience and do a good job of work.'

'If it's only your work you're interested in, that's all to the good,' he said. 'I seem to have been wasting my breath. I'm sorry.' But he didn't look sorry. It was difficult to think of him as ever being humble. He was too essentially masculine and arrogant.

She had quite decided now she didn't like him. He had done everything in his power to prick the glowing bubble of her happiness in the new life she was about to enter. But she was determined to disregard all he had said. Mark had assured her she would be happy in her working and her social life in New York. She had the prospect of the exciting reunion with her mother. What if a girl named Coleen Hausman and Mark were old friends? What if their names had even been coupled together in the gossip columns? She knew that gossip columnists could dream up stories that had no truth in them whatsoever. She was confident that Mark would have told her had he been engaged or seriously involved with another girl. She told herself she had complete confidence in Mark. She wasn't going to let this objectionable man upset her.

She smiled across at him coldly. 'Now that you've told me all the pitfalls which may await me in New York, couldn't we talk of something more pleasant?'

He chuckled. 'I can see you're still mad at me. Maybe I've said more than I should have said. But you seem a nice sort of girl — innocent, in a way naïve. I couldn't let you walk straight into danger without trying to do something about it. I'll be around. If you want me, you may call upon me. You may not think so at the moment, but I'm your friend, Janet. If you ever find yourself in a tight spot, just call upon me. I'll do my best to help you out.'

# 4

After that, ordinary conversation had been difficult. He had made no further reference to her journey to the United States. He talked instead about Australia, his impressions of it, and more than once he asked for her opinion. He told her that in some respects the Australian way of life was similar to the American way of life, but there were some sharp differences. The American way of life was more competitive; men were keener on their jobs, more anxious to hold them down, more fearful of losing them. They hadn't the free-and-easy spirit the Australians had. If an Australian lost his job he didn't seem to give a damn; he was confident of finding another the next day. America wasn't like that; men were dead scared of losing their jobs, especially in the artistic profession. Another job didn't come so easily. It made them harder in business, though on the surface they were essentially a sentimental nation.

'The boss will weep, over the death of your child and fire you the next moment,' Julian Gaden had said. 'I've said it before and I'll say it again — if I were you, Janet I'd think more than once about leaving this country.'

'Please,' she begged. 'We've talked quite enough about that as it is. This is a wonderful opportunity Mark is giving me and I'm quite determined to take full advantage of it.' And to change the conversation, she asked, 'What are you going to do for the rest of your time in Australia?'

'I thought of taking a trip up to Surfers' Paradise,' he said. 'I've heard some mighty fine things about it. If you weren't Mark Dexter's friend, I'd suggest that you and I take the trip together — strictly platonic, of course.'

She smiled. 'I might have taken you up on that. I've always wanted to see Surfers' Paradise myself, but I have so many things to see to before we leave for the States.'

He laughed a little ruefully. 'Then I might as well have been talking into a vacuum.'

'I told you before I have every intention of taking advantage of this opportunity,' she said.

Finally they left the restaurant and he took her home.

'Do you ask me inside for a final drink?' he suggested. 'I'll even settle for that rather too sweet sherry.'

She laughed. 'I won't ask you in tonight, Julian. It's late; we might disturb the girls.'

'Do I merit a kiss? Or are all your kisses reserved for Mark Dexter?' He drew her hand in his and tried to pull her closer to him.

She jerked away from him.

'My kisses are not reserved for Mark, but they are reserved for whom I choose to give them to.'

He raised that dark untidy eyebrow again. 'And I don't merit a kiss? Not even after giving you a swell dinner?'

She shook her head. 'No. Thank you for it all the same.'

'But you don't thank me for the advice I gave you?'

'No, I don't thank you for that. I think I am quite capable of taking care of my own affairs, Mr. Gaden.'

'Well as I said, I'll be seeing you. Maybe in New York, maybe sooner. You called me Mr. Gaden just then. I thought we were friends.'

'I thought so too, until you started trying to interfere in my life.'

'I'll let you go your own sweet wilful way. I may be on hand to pick up the pieces. Good night again.' He went from her down the steps.

She thought, as she let herself into the house with her latch-key, what a curious man he was. In certain moods he was undeniably attractive. He was essentially masculine, with a touch of arrogance. How came he to be so interested in her affairs? All evening she had felt him looking her over as though she were a specimen under a microscope. It had discomfited her and many of his remarks had made her furious. What had it to do with him whether she went to New York or stayed out here in Sydney? The advice he had given her was mere presumption on his part. What if Mark was friends with a girl named Coleen Hausman? She couldn't have expected him to have gone through life without having any girl friends. Coleen's father might be a millionaire, but did that really matter? Mark seemed to have plenty for his own needs. Would he want a wife simply because she was the daughter of a millionaire?

She tossed and turned in bed; she had difficulty in getting to sleep that night. But she was quite determined that nothing Julian had said would make any difference to her present arrangements. She was still just as eager to go to the States; and even if Mark's Café Society set wouldn't accept her, she would have her mother and her mother's friends. A penthouse apartment like a palace — he had described it. Unwillingly the nagging thought came — why hadn't her mother ever invited her over there? If Tim and she were as rich as Julian seemed to infer, her mother could easily have sent her the money for the passage. Didn't she want to see her? Was this idea of surprising her such a good idea? Mightn't it be better if she cabled her she was coming?

She decided to do just that before she finally fell asleep. She cabled her the next morning and spent the following day in a fever of excitement for the answer to come. She was disquieted and dismayed at the reply when it finally came. It read: 'VERY RUSHED WITH BUSINESS AT THE MOMENT WHY NOT POSTPONE YOUR VISIT FOR A LITTLE.' It was signed, 'YOUR SISTER JUNE.'

She was more than disquieted; she was deeply hurt. She couldn't help remembering the advice Julian had given her. He had warned her definitely against this visit to the United States. He had even mentioned danger. But she had her visa for the next six months and Mark had already arranged their aeroplane reservations. Curiously, her hurt at her mother's reply made her more than ever determined upon going. Anyhow, she had no job here, and the prospect of a job awaiting her in New York was undeniably exciting.

Was her mother afraid the relationship between them would leak out? Why should she deny her own daughter?

She cabled back an angry reply: 'AM COMING ANYHOW JOB AWAITING ME SHAN'T GET IN YOUR HAIR.' She added a final facetious touch: 'YOUR SISTER JANET.'

* * *

She finished up at the Hamilton Press the following week. Alvin Harvey had somewhat recovered from his ill-temper. He looked at her sadly. 'I could have given you a good life if you'd stayed out here, Janet. Marriage isn't everything.'

'I believe in marriage,' Janet replied. 'When I marry, I hope it will be for keeps. I would never consider any other arrangement. Besides, I couldn't have borne to hurt Edith as we should have done.'

'She needn't have known,' he said. 'But after all, it's your own life to live. I hoped there was a place in it for me. I'm sorry I was mistaken.'

'I'm sorry you even thought of such a thing.' She added more gently, 'Good-bye, Alvin. Try to be content with your wife and family. You've got a truly marvellous family.'

'I know.' He shook his head. 'But a man of my age gets ideas.'

'If I may presume to say so, keep your ideas for your work and love for your family. Good-bye, Alvin, and thank you for all you've done for me while I've been working here.'

'You should thank me for the

introduction I gave you to Mark Dexter. Are you going to marry him, Janet?'

'There's no idea of marriage. I'm going over purely on a job.'

He looked up at her from under his hooded brows from where he sat before his desk. 'But you like him, don't you?'

'Yes,' she admitted. 'I like him very much.' A voice whispered in her heart, 'Too much. Too much for my own good.' But aloud she merely said, 'Good-bye, and thank you again, Alvin.'

# 5

The jet plane which carried Janet and Mark on their journey to New York reached the Fijian Islands in the first flush of a riotous sunset. Janet had never seen any sunset to compare with it. As the plane lost height they could see clearly the group of two hundred and fifty coral islands which make up the Fijian group. They had taken on the blood-red colour of the sunset.

Presently they could distinguish the palm trees which crept right down to the water's edge. They could see the little beaches which were curving strips of gold. Janet caught her breath in wonderment. 'I've never seen anything like it,' she whispered to Mark. 'It's out of this world.'

He nodded and asked, 'You're happy, Janet? You have no regrets about leaving Sydney?'

She shook her head and laughed. 'None whatsoever. I feel this plane is like a magic carpet. We are going to see so many places I've only dreamt about. I've always wanted to travel in the Pacific; I've never had the opportunity.'

'We land on the main island, Viti Levu,' Mark leant across to say to her. 'The airport is Nadi. I wish we had the time to drive into Suva — that's the capital. But it's a hundred or so miles along the coast. We only have three hours here. Time to get dinner before pushing off again.'

Presently she could see the coral reef which fringed the shoreline. The red of the sunset had faded, but the gold intermingled with the encroaching grey. Soon they were over the airport, a large group of sprawling buildings from which welcoming lights flowed out into the evening mist.

The plane made a perfect landing. It was a relief to get out and stretch their limbs. As they walked across the tarmac toward the brilliantly lit reception hall,

Janet had her first sight of a Fijian policeman. He was a truly magnificent specimen of manhood, tall, well-built, dark-skinned, with a mop of fuzzy hair. He was dressed in a short navy tunic, and instead of trousers he wore the native *sulu*, like a short white skirt.

'Are all the natives as strong and tall as he is?' she asked Mark.

He smiled. 'The Fijians are a very fine race of men. They are highly intelligent, too. I stopped over here a couple of days on my way to Sydney and drove round the island. It's picturesque and colourful. I wish we could see more of it now, but I have to hurry back; plenty of business awaits me in New York. I'm afraid I'm going to keep you very busy, Janet.'

She smiled. 'I'll welcome that. If you keep me busy enough, I won't feel strange and lonely.'

He drew her arm through his as they walked towards the reception hall. His dark grey eyes smiled down into her face. 'I'll do my best to see you're not lonely, Janet. You've been such a good friend to me in Sydney, I'll try and be an equally good friend to you in New York.'

'I shall never cease to thank you for giving me this marvellous opportunity,' she told him.

'I only hope you'll never regret it.' His voice was serious and intent. 'In these past weeks you've come to mean quite a lot to me, Janet.'

Her heart lifted and started beating rapidly. The touch of his hand thrilled her. The sense of excitement remained with her as they entered the pleasant reception hall, furnished with thick rush mats, flat Fijian couches, bamboo furniture, and the native tapestry made from Mulberry bark. A small cheerful bar stood at one corner of the room. The bar-tender was coloured, his hair as thick and fuzzy as the policeman's had been. The air was hot and steamy.

'What about a cool drink?' Mark suggested.

The bar-tender cheerfully made them

two lime squashes.

Mark glanced at his wrist-watch. 'There is still a good hour before they'll be serving dinner. Did you take my suggestion and slip a bathing suit into your overnight bag?'

She nodded. 'I did.'

'Good. Let's go for a swim in that little beach down yonder. There's an overnight hotel at the airport. We can change there.'

'A swim would be wonderful,' she said. 'So very refreshing.'

Up at the hotel the reception clerk, another Fijian, smilingly showed them rooms in which they could change. The twilight still lingered though the moon was rising. The sand still felt hot under their bare feet. The beach was screened by palm trees. There was no one but themselves on the beach.

They ran hand in hand across the sand into the darkening waters. The sea was deliciously cool. They felt like children on a stolen holiday. They frollicked in the water, splashing each other, and then they swam side by side out to the coral reef. They rested a while on the reef. The moon was full now and the stars were showing. They rested in the water, shoulder to shoulder, their bodies touching. This surely was paradise, Janet thought.

'I was here swimming before, but it wasn't like this,' Mark said presently. 'You must be a witch, Janet. You have the power to change everything. May I kiss you, Janet?'

Their wet bodies clung together as he kissed her. She had a tense emotional feeling as though she were poised on top of the world.

'You're coming to mean something pretty big in my life,' he said softly. 'Do you like me, Janet?'

She gave a small muffled laugh. 'Oh, yes, I like you, Mark.'

'That's good,' he said.

Suddenly she was remembering what Julian Gaden had said to her.

'You must have plenty of friends in New York, Mark. You mustn't worry too much about me. I'll be all right.'

'But I want to look after you,' he told her. 'My friends will be glad to accept you amongst them.'

But Julian had said otherwise. What was the truth?

Presently they swam back to shore, went hand in hand up through the moonlit darkness to the hotel, where they changed again into their travelling clothes.

The restaurant where they would dine adjoined the reception room at the airport terminal. As they passed the small bar, Mark stopped. 'I could use a drink now, a fairly stiff one,' he said. 'What about you?'

'I feel lazy and happy,' she said. 'Perhaps I do need something to pep me up.'

'A rum cocktail is always good after a swim,' he said.

They seated themselves on two high stools and the grinning bar-tender with the fuzzy black hair greeted them as if they were old friends. They toasted each other, his dark grey eyes smiling directly down into her bright hazel ones. 'This is surely going to be the best air trip I've ever taken in my life,' he said softly.

'We stop next at Canton Island, but there's nothing to see there, just a strip of land in the middle of the sea. But then Honolulu; there we have a five-hour break. I'm longing to show you Honolulu, Janet.'

She looked about her. 'But nothing could really be nicer than this.'

'Just wait until you've seen Honolulu,' he said. 'The Royal Hawaiian Hotel and Waikiki Beach. Who knows, we might even arrange a stop-over there.'

'That would be wonderful,' she said. 'But I thought your work in New York was pressing.'

'Nothing in New York seems of such pressing importance after tonight,' he said in that same soft intent voice. 'You did something to me when you kissed me out there on the reef, Janet; something I never want to forget.'

It was all perfect — too perfect. Janet realised that a few moments later, when a well-known voice said, 'Well, look who's here! But then since I'm catching your plane it's not all that much of a coincidence, is it?'

They both turned simultaneously. Julian Gaden was standing there, grinning at them in his lopsided way, his deep blue eyes twinkling with merriment, not untinged with maliciousness.

'Have a round on me,' he said as they said nothing at all. 'What's the matter with you? Have you both lost your tongues?'

'You took us by surprise,' Mark finally said. 'I thought you'd left for the States some time back.'

'I wanted to see this place,' he said. 'So when I got back to Sydney I hopped on a plane and flew over to here. I've been here a week, taking a ride around the island, stopping off at various places. This place has charm but it isn't up-to-date; it's completely unspoiled. But now I must be getting home, so I booked on your plane.'

As he talked he took a seat beside them at the bar. He went on talking pleasantly and cheerfully. He didn't seem to understand that he wasn't wanted. Definitely as far as Janet was concerned, he wasn't wanted. His presence on the plane would spoil the thrill of being alone with Mark. She told herself she had never liked him; now she thought she almost hated him.

'And how are you enjoying your trip, Janet?' he asked. 'Sorry I didn't get to look you up again when I was passing through Sydney, but I wasn't sure whether or not you'd welcome a visit from me.'

'I'm enjoying myself very well,' Janet remarked, ignoring the last half of his remark.

'We're just going in to have dinner,' Mark said presently. 'See you on the plane, Julian.'

He didn't invite Julian to join them for dinner, and Janet was glad. But for some reason the dinner wasn't the enchanting meal it should have been after that swim and that close embrace out on the coral reef. The appearance of the tall lean American with the long nose, the hard jaw and high cheekbones, the untidy black hair, seemed to have spoiled some of the enchantment for them. Janet was remembering his warning to her.

Dash it all, why need he have joined them on this special plane? Had it been mere coincidence or had his action been deliberate? But why should he want to follow them around? He might have known Mark casually in New York, but he had nothing whatever to do with her.

She decided it must have been a coincidence after all. But what an unfortunate coincidence!

The food was plain good British cooking such as you find at almost every outpost of the Commonwealth. There were no national Fijian dishes served.

'But wait until we get to Honolulu,' Mark said, 'and you eat the delicious pig cooked in an *imu*, which is an underground oven composed mainly of hot stones. The pig is wrapped in ti-leaves. It is really one of the most succulent dishes I've ever tasted.'

'I'd love to try it. You're like a magician, Mark, opening up a whole new world for me. I feel like Cinderella at the Prince's ball.'

He laughed and said, 'You don't look like Cinderella, not the Cinderella in rags, anyhow. The Fairy Godmother did a very good job on you. But don't kid yourself I'm not enjoying this as much as you are. As I said before, it's a simply splendid trip. I only wish,' he added in an undertone, 'that fellow Julian Gaden hadn't turned up. He doesn't belong to the same set I move in in New York, but he used to be a great friend of Coleen Hausman's late husband.'

Julian had mention Coleen Hausman to her, but this was the first time Mark had mentioned her. She decided to play the innocent.

'Who is Coleen Hausman, Mark?'

'A great friend,' he said. 'She and I were practically brought up together. We had a teenage love affair and then almost in the midst of it she eloped with Henry Hausman.' He gave a wry grin and added, 'I was pretty much cut up at the time, but now I'm able to laugh about it. We were only kids. Coleen laughs about it with me. We're great friends.'

Julian had warned her about Mark's friendship with Coleen Hausman.

'Was the marriage a success?' she asked.

He gave a small shake of his head. 'Not much of a success, I'm afraid. Henry drank and gambled, and there were other women. Finally he got himself smashed up in a motor accident. But Julian Gaden was a great friend of his.'

'So Mrs. Hausman is now a gay young widow.'

'Coleen was always gay,' he said. 'Even when she was going through the worst periods of her marriage. You'll meet her in New York. You'll like her.'

'I hope she'll like me,' Janet said.

'You bet she will.'

But Julian had hinted there were several reasons why Coleen Hausman shouldn't particularly like her. Who was she to believe?

She glanced across the dining-room. Julian was dining by himself at a small table in the corner. At the moment he was pushing back a lock of dark hair which flopped untidily across his forehead. His face was serious; it looked almost grim. Had he been hurt they hadn't invited him to join them? He stood out in that company of casual tourists; he was so long and lean, and his features, though not strictly handsome, were arresting looking. The hard jaw seemed especially prominent at that moment.

He caught her glance and his deep blue eyes looked directly across at her.

She felt a faint flush rise to her cheeks, which was absurd. She hastily looked away from him.

They discovered when they boarded the plane that Julian was seated directly across the aisle from them. She wished he had been seated further back in the plane. They had to keep up a semblance of friendliness.

'That damned fellow always seems to be on my ear,' Mark said in an undertone. 'I wish to heaven he'd booked himself on another plane.'

It was a starful night; the moon shone down on the group of Fijian Islands. The small curves of the beaches looked silver in the moonlight and the palms which surrounded them were black shapes, almost menacing. But soon they were high up in the clouds and the hostess and steward were making preparations for the night. The hostess lowered the backs of their seats so that they could recline comfortably. She asked if they would like tea or coffee before retiring. She handed each of them a rug and pillow.

Some of the women had gone into the toilet and changed into dressing-gowns, but Janet felt she was too close to Mark. It might be embarrassing. She kicked off her shoes and loosened the skirt belt of her travelling suit. She slipped off the jacket and pulled the rug up higher.

Mark had also loosened his belt and taken off his shoes. He leant back and said, 'I hope you sleep well, Janet dear.' One of his hands reached out and pressed hers warmly. 'I'm tired after that swim,' he added. 'I think I'll sleep. I hope you'll do the same.' He turned his head on the pillow and smiled at her. 'Good night. Sweet dreams.' He was asleep almost immediately.

But Janet stayed awake for a long time. There was sufficient light for her to see him clearly. He looked boyishly handsome asleep. She would have liked to reach out her hand and touch his face, caressing it lingeringly. His head slipped sideways so that it almost rested upon her shoulder. His light brown hair had a greyish tinge in that light. Mark would always be handsome. She sensed he would not lose his looks with the years, but become even handsomer as he grew older. He was young to have such a responsible position. She hoped she would be able to help him. She would do her darned best to help him in every way she could. She had so much to thank him for — this wonderful trip; the opportunity of working in New York. He had kissed her, but how much did he really like her? Surely he must like her a lot to have given her this magnificent opportunity.

She wished she could lean across and kiss him softly on the check and whisper, 'Thank you.'

She glanced across the aisle to where Julian Gaden was sleeping. His tall lean frame was sprawled out loosely and untidily. She had the curious feeling that even though he slept he was very much alert; he could waken on the moment and be very wide awake. Mark looked like a handsome boy asleep, but Julian had nothing boyish about him; he was very much the arrogant masculine male, even in his sleep.

She looked away from him and forced herself to close her eyes. She must try and get some sleep. If she didn't, she would look a wreck in the morning, and she wanted to look nice, especially nice — for Mark.

She must have slept finally, for when she awakened it was dawn, the sky was blood-red and crimson. No one yet was stirring, but she felt cramped from the unnatural position. Last night Mark had shown her the small observation lounge in the back of the plane. She decided to go out there and sit and watch the dawn break. She felt wide awake; there was no possibility of further sleep.

She stopped in at the ladies' toilet to wash her face, re-do her make-up and comb her hair. Her longish copper-coloured hair fell attractively to her shoulders, curling in. Her face was still flushed from her sleep, but her hazel eyes were bright.

She made her way quietly to the observation lounge with two couches and a table heaped with magazines. She had expected to be alone in the observation lounge at this early hour; she hoped to be alone. But as she entered the lounge she saw Julian's long lean figure with his back turned to her, staring out into the sunrise. She had half a mind to turn and leave, but he must have heard her enter, for at that moment he swung round.

He grinned her a welcome. 'Come to share the sunrise with me? That's nice. It's a beautiful sight, and like all beautiful things in this world, it should be shared.'

'I thought when I passed you you were sound asleep.'

'But I heard you pass. I sleep very lightly. I can be awake on the instant.'

So she had been right in her impression of him the evening before.

They both stood and looked out on to where the dawn, a riot of glorious colours, was breaking on the horizon.

'Enjoying your trip, Janet?' he asked her.

'Very much.'

He raised one of his untidy eyebrows. 'It has come up to all your expectations?'

She nodded again. 'More, much more.'

'You certainly gave me the brush-off last night,' he said. 'You might have invited me to share your dinner table.'

'That was up to Mark. I'm his guest.'

He grinned again, his long lean face slipping sideways. 'I think I'm beginning to get in the boy friend's hair. He wasn't pleased that I joined your plane.'

She felt emboldened to ask, 'Was it pure coincidence that made you join this plane, Mr. Gaden?'

'I thought we'd agreed that you call me Julian?' he said. 'This plane was leaving about the time I wanted to leave the island. I'd seen enough. The coastline is a dream, the villages are primitive and picturesque. The native Fijians are magnificent specimens, but the islands are cluttered up as well with Indians and Chinese. They are the chief traders. But I'll admit I had a yen to see you again, Janet. I haven't seen much of you, but you've made quite a hit with me, young lady.'

'Even though I refused to take your advice and stay back in Sydney?'

'Even so. It shows you have courage — maybe foolhardy courage. I warned you, didn't I, that you might be stepping into an unpleasant situation?'

'You also used the word 'danger',' she reminded him. 'That seems to me sheer nonsense.'

'Maybe,' he said, and then he asked abruptly, 'Has Mark mentioned Coleen Hausman to you?'

She was faintly startled by the abrupt question.

'Yes, he mentioned her last night at dinner. He said that he and she were great friends, they had practically been brought up together. He said the man she married, who was killed in a car smash, wasn't any good.'

'He said *that*?' Julian's voice was half incredulous.

'I believe he drank and gambled. Mark said something about other women.'

'That's a downright lie,' Julian said angrily. 'Henry Hausman happened to be one of my best friends. He may have gambled a little on the horses, but then most rich young men do, but I swear he never drank to excess. And as for other women, that's sheer nonsense. He was nuts about Coleen. Everything Mark said to you about Henry Hausman is a pack of lies.' His voice was hard and furious; his jaw jutted out; his blue eyes were hard, there was menace in them.

'Coleen has been feeding Mark a grand story,' he went on more quietly. 'She married Henry on a purely physical attraction and then quickly tired of him. If he drank at all, it was because of her, her complete indifference to him. If she had any cause to divorce him, she would have done so. But he gave her no cause. And it was strange to think that Henry was killed in a car smash. He was one of the best drivers I've ever known. I've always thought there was something fishy about that accident.'

She was appalled.

'You mean the accident mightn't have been a genuine accident?'

'I'm not saying anything,' Julian said. 'I'm keeping my mouth shut. But that doesn't prevent my thinking things.'

'It's queer that you were such a friend of Coleen's husband and know my sister's husband as well.'

'It isn't so queer,' he said. 'I make it my job to get about, to meet people likely to make the news. Your sister, Madame June's Beauty Salon is very much in the news. As I told you, most of the socialites go to her for beauty treatment.'

The dawn was bright about them

now. What he had told her was disturbing. Mark had said that Coleen Hausman and he were nothing but friends. Was that the complete truth?

The passengers on the plane were stirring. The steward was busy making tea and coffee, which the hostess handed round. She came into the observation lounge to ask if they would like juice first before their tea and coffee. 'We serve breakfast in an hour,' she said.

Mark might be awake and wondering where she was.

'I think I'll go back to my seat now,' she said to Julian.

'You don't like what I've been telling you,' he said.

She made a small wry grimace. 'I never like the things you tell me. I don't know why you bother.'

'I said I liked you. Have you forgotten? I don't want you to get into a mess if I can help it.'

'I wish you wouldn't concern yourself about me at all,' she said.

'You may think that now. But I have a feeling that some day — and it may be pretty soon — you may be glad your Uncle Julian was around.' He grinned at her again. 'Happy eating.'

# 6

They stopped briefly at Canton Island to refuel. They were served coffee and sandwiches in the airport reception house.

The airport reception house was an attractive spot on that lonely strip of island — surely one of the loneliest outposts in the world. From the outside it looked like an attractive bungalow with a wide veranda and a neat well-kept garden in front. Inside, the rooms were airy and tastefully furnished with wicker furniture and rush mats.

Janet was fascinated with a large glass case at one end of the room in which was an amazing collection of sea shells of every variety. They were all shapes and sizes and colours and glittered as though they were so many jewels.

Afterwards Mark and she went

outside for a stroll. They hadn't seen Julian since they left the aeroplane.

'I wonder what the fellows who work here feel like,' Mark mused. 'It must be damned lonely for them. Almost like being in a prison.'

There was a strip of beach and a few palm trees, but most of the island was flat and bare.

'What were you and Julian Gaden talking about in the observation lounge this morning?' he asked her.

'You knew we were there? I thought you were asleep.'

'When I awoke you were gone and Julian's seat was also empty. I put two and two together.'

'Why didn't you come out and join us?'

'I thought I might be intruding.' His voice was slightly stiff.

'Oh, Mark, surely you didn't think that after all you've done for me!'

'I don't want your gratitude.' His voice was still slightly stiff. 'Bringing you over to the States was a business proposition.

As you know, I want you to work on those Australian manuscripts for me.'

She felt a sense of bleakness. Was that the only reason he had wanted her to come to New York — just to work over those Australian manuscripts? Last night at Nadi their wet bodies had clung together, they had kissed. He had said she had come to mean something very important in his life. Now all at once he made the whole trip seem like a business proposition.

'You don't like Julian, do you?' she said.

'Not particularly. But you seem to like him. You went out to dine with him one night in Sydney. And then this morning you were in the observation lounge together.'

'I didn't think you'd mind me dining with him in Sydney,' she said. 'It was only once. And this morning, that we were both in the observation lounge together was a pure coincidence. Please believe me, Mark.' Her voice was near to tears.

His expression softened. 'It may have been quite innocent on your part, Janet — this morning I mean — but I can't accept it as a coincidence that he should have joined this special flight. He must have known we'd be on board. I think that man has a yen for you, my darling.' The 'my darling' must have slipped out, for he flushed deeply afterwards.

But her heart lightened. She felt almost dizzy with joy. So whatever he had said, she did mean more to him than merely an extra member he was adding to his firm.

'We'd better be getting back to the airport,' he said finally. The pause had been long and awkward.

They walked back to the bungalow reception house in silence. Did he regret what he had let slip out? Was he afraid she might take advantage of it?

They took their seats again in the plane. Once they were airborne Julian leant over to them and said, 'I didn't see you on the island. But then I went for a walk. These long legs of mine need stretching. I wonder how the personnel at the airport feel each time a plane takes off? Don't they wish that they themselves were going back to civilisation? They must lead a very lonely life.'

'Mark and I were saying the same thing,' Janet said.

'Well our next stop is Honolulu,' he smiled. 'And that isn't a lonely place, for sure.'

On the long flight to Honolulu they passed through a thunderstorm. The plane dropped sharply and quivered in the air. After that it went on in jerky jumps. Janet tried not to be afraid, but she was trembling. Mark took her hand and held it closely. 'Don't be afraid, Janet,' he said softly.

'I'm trying not to be,' she said, but she could almost hear her own teeth chattering.

She glanced rather wildly about her and happened to meet Julian's eyes across the aisle. His face, which was usually set in rather hard lines, broke into a grin. He raised a hand to her in a half salute. For some reason she felt less scared afterwards and presently they were through the storm and the hostess was serving coffee as though she felt the passengers needed it to soothe their nerves.

'These air hostesses are really marvellous,' she said to Mark. 'Whatever happens, they keep on smiling. They make one ashamed of oneself for being scared. They're so pretty and efficient, and without any sense of familiarity they treat us all as though we were friends.'

'No wonder so many of them get married,' Mark retorted. 'The airline give them an intensive training, and then, as often as not, within a year they're married. If I was the manager of an airline, I'd make them sign some sort of contract that they remain in the service of the airline for a certain period of years.'

'But that would be scarcely fair to them,' Janet protested. 'If they should fall in love, of course they would want to marry.'

'You think marriage so important?' Mark asked quietly. 'Isn't love important in itself? Must love always race into marriage?'

Alvin Harvey had said much the same thing to her in his office when she said goodbye to him. It disquietened her to hear Mark say it. Love and marriage were synonymous in her mind. You fell in love; after a short space of time you married. But perhaps that was entirely feminine reaction; perhaps men didn't feel like that. Mark was twenty-seven or -eight, and he had never married. And yet there must have been other girls besides Coleen Hausman in his life. He was so attractive, so considerate, so desirable in every way. Was she a fool to hope that one day he would ask her to become his wife? Had he made love to many girls, kissed them as he kissed her that night on the coral reef? Had he called many girls 'my darling?'

The hostess was serving lunch, though, having already had coffee and sandwiches at Canton Island, they had little appetite for it.

It was mid-morning on the day they reached the Hawaiian Islands. As they lost height and the islands came into view they seemed fantastically lovely. The lush green of the islands with the purple hills rising in the centre, the bright blue sea shading to paler blue behind the coral reef, the roads which looked like ribbons twisting between smaller islands.

Janet caught her breath. 'I don't think I've ever seen anything more beautiful in all my life.'

Mark agreed that it was beautiful. 'I've flown over the Hawaiian Islands at least a dozen times,' he told her. 'Honolulu is a spot I've often chosen for a holiday. You see that big island down there? That's the largest — Hawaii. And those high mountain peaks you see rising in the centre are Nauna Los and Mauna Kea. Both of them are as high as many mountains in the Swiss Alps. Can you see that cluster of buildings? That's Hilo, the principal city. It's beautiful and spectacular, but it's never attracted the tourist as Honolulu does. But then Honolulu has a myraid of luxury tourist hotels and the famous Waikiki Beach.'

'I can't wait to get there,' Janet said. 'To visit places like this is what I've always longed to do.'

Mark laughed his pleasant, good-natured laugh. 'You're a stimulating companion, Janet. You make me enjoy everything as intensely as you enjoy it yourself. But then you have so much verve, so much enthusiasm. In certain sets in the States it's the fashion to be bored.'

She laughed too. 'Then you're certainly not in the fashion, Mark. Look how much you enjoyed my showing you the sights around Sydney — the beaches at Deewhy, Avalon and Palm Beach, and that wonderful trip we took up into the Blue Mountains. I can swear you weren't bored.'

'No, I wasn't bored. But then I had you along with me, Janet. As I said before, you're a most stimulating companion You give me the same enthusiasm about things as you have yourself. That's one reason I like you so very much.'

He had used the word 'like.' She could have wished he had used a stronger word. But she had schooled herself to wait. She sensed that Mark wasn't a man to rush into anything.

Finally they circled above Honolulu and made a perfect landing on the airstrip. Going through the Customs and showing their passports was a mere formality, and directly they stepped out of the Customs shed, what a colourful scene it was. Half the town seemed to have come down to welcome the new arrivals. There were hula girls in native costume, who threw flower leis of plumeria, sweet-smelling ginger and jasmine around their necks. There were native Hawaiian women, dark-skinned and aristocratic looking, wearing their holokulas, a loose-fitting garment with a small train. You could see Japanese and Chinese faces, and also the suntanned faces of American visitors to the island.

One of these pushed her way through the crowd towards them. She was a strikingly lovely girl, tallish, with a perfectly shaped face and fair hair that shone golden in the sunlight. As she came closer, Janet saw that her eyes were as blue as the waters inside the coral reef.

'Mark, darling,' she said, and flung herself upon him.

Mark seemed completely taken by surprise. 'Why, Coleen!' he exclaimed. 'What ever brings you here to Honolulu?'

'I came to be a welcoming party of one.' She smiled up at him. 'I was bored with New York and thought I'd fly across and meet your plane. I've been here several days, as a matter of fact. What fun it is to see you again.'

'It was darned decent of you to come all this way to meet me, Coleen.' He disentangled himself from her clinging arms. He looked embarrassed. 'I want you to meet Janet Freeman. She's coming over to assist us in the office.'

'Oh.' Coleen's voice was faintly startled. 'I didn't know you were bringing over an assistant as well as a stack of manuscripts, Mark.'

'Janet was so helpful to me in Sydney, I thought we needed her in the office. This is Janet Freeman — Coleen Hausman.'

'Hi, Janet,' Coleen said, and the two girls shook hands.

Janet found herself being looked over very appraisingly, very shrewdly. Those dreamy blue eyes could be very intent.

She resents my being here, Janet thought. She hoped to have Mark all to herself.

'I'm staying at the Royal Hawaiian,' Coleen said. 'I have one of their lovely *lanai* suites, looking right over Waikiki Beach. I hoped I could persuade you to stop over for a few days, Mark, so that we could enjoy a brief holiday in this glorious place.'

Mark had once suggested the same thing to *her*, Janet thought.

'Couldn't you send Janet on ahead? Please, Mark.' She smiled at him bewitchingly.

Janet gathered that this rich, lovely girl was used to having her own way in everything.

''Fraid it can't be managed,' Mark said, frowning. 'I have to get back to the office, Coleen.'

She pouted. But even when she pouted her small gaminlike face looked attractive.

'Oh, Mark, you're surely not going to disappoint me?'

'Afraid I have to, Coleen.'

She looped her arm prettily through his. 'Well come along to the Royal Hawaiian now. We have time to have a swim before luncheon.'

She had ignored Janet completely in the invitation. Obviously she was determined to treat her as Mark had introduced her — just another member of the office staff. Janet sensed that in this girl she had a strong potential rival. She might have ditched Mark once to marry Henry Hausman on an impulse, but Mark was now obviously the chief man in her thoughts.

Julian had warned her about Coleen Hausman, but Mark had assured her they were merely friends. He had implied that the romance they had had in their teens was now very much a thing of the past. But was it?

'You'll come along with us, won't you, Janet?' he said. He added to Coleen; 'I promised to show Janet Honolulu. This is the first time she's been out of Australia.'

Coleen gave in gracefully. 'Of course, come along with us, Miss Freeman. You'll be thrilled with Honolulu. It's the most exciting place. How long are you stopping over, Mark?'

'I was asked to check up at the airways office in the Royal Hawaiian at lunch-time,' he said. 'It seems, from what I overhead, the plane suffered a little damage in that storm we flew through.'

'Let's hope the old plane suffered serious damage and you can make a really long stop-over, Mark.'

Like so many women in Hawaii, as well as wearing an orchid lei she had orchids in her hair. When she walked she seemed rather to float; her every movement was graceful.

She had a taxi waiting and they all climbed in, Janet and Mark carrying their overnight bags. After the brilliant scene at the airport, Janet found the town itself slightly disappointing. The shopping centre was crowded and unspectacular. Already the heat was intense; you could see the perspiration standing out on the faces of the people. Such a mixed conglomeration of faces — pale-skinned American faces, Japanese faces, Chinese, dark-skinned Hawaiians with their aristocratic-looking features. The native Hawaiians were certainly a spectacular race of people. But once you passed the rather undistinguished business centre, you were once again enchanted. Flowers were everywhere — in the gardens of the rich-looking bungalows, native women were making leis of jasmine, ginger, plumeria and orchids on the streets. There were flowering trees of every colour in the bungalows — or *hales*, as Mark told her they were called. Flowering shrubs of every colour; bougainvillea, hibiscus, exotic orchids growing almost wild, and as well there was the spectacular bird of paradise flower. All the women were dressed in Mother Hubbards of backless dresses of exotic colours. The men's patterned aloha shirts were equally exotic. The crowd swarmed from the pavements on to the roads, laughing and talking; everyone and everything moved at a leisurely pacc, as seemed right in this island which was given over almost entirely to pleasure.

As they drove down Kalia Road,

Mark pointed out to Janet the various famous big hotels. Coleen laughed at him and said, 'You sound like a professional guide, Mark.'

'I want Janet to see as much as possible in the short time she's here.'

'I remember Henry and I nearly joined you once, but Henry was in no shape to make the trip,' Coleen said.

'I remember.' Mark's face clouded over slightly. 'I was disappointed that you couldn't come.'

'But I'm sure you found other feminine attractions,' Coleen laughed back at him. 'You are really by way of being a lady-killer, Mark. I hope Miss Freeman doesn't take your attentions seriously.'

It was said good-humouredly, but there was a sting behind the words. Janet had a sudden sense of despair. How could she hope to compete with this brilliant lovely socialite, whom Mark had known ever since their childhood and had once loved?

The cab drew up before the Royal

Hawaiian Hotel. It was a most impressive hotel, right on the waterfront and facing Waikiki Beach. As they crossed the foyer, or *lanai*, she could see down the long corridor on to the beach. She could see the famous out-rigger boats, manned by six, which rode the surf waves. She could see the crowds gathered on the beaches, the Lilos, the colourful sun umbrellas. The lounge itself was very spacious. She found herself staring at a fine exhibition of white and rose-tinted coral. And in a shop down the corridor, a magnificent display of flowers.

'Would you like to come to my suite and tidy up?' Coleen invited Janet. 'You have your bathing suit in your overnight bag, I hope. We could change at once and then go straight down on to the beach. We can get a cool drink at the Outrigger Club. They serve delightful lunches and you needn't change. What do you say we lunch there, Mark?'

'It sounds a splendid idea,' he said.

'Once we've changed, you could

change in my suite, Mark,' she said. 'While you're changing we'll go down on to the beach and wait for you there.'

Coleen's *lanai* suite was certainly a delightful place. There was a bedroom, sitting-room and a large balcony which looked down upon the beach. The rooms themselves were full of flowers — bowls of flowers. Their fragrance filled the air. It was difficult for Janet to believe such luxury as this existed.

She changed in the shower-room, leaving the bedroom to Coleen.

Coleen wore a strapless bathing suit of the same deep blue colour as her eyes. She wore golden sandals, showing the toe nails that were painted the same shade of red as her long fingernails. Her beach robe was of pale gold.

Janet felt somewhat inadequate beside her. She wished now she had bought a new swimsuit before she left Sydney. She had no wrap, but Coleen lent her one. It was emerald-green and complemented the deep copper shade of Janet's hair.

'Mark is a very charming person, isn't he?' Coleen commented as she stood before the mirror putting some last-minute touches to her skilfully applied make-up.

Since Mark and she had been playmates in their youth, she must have been twenty-four or -five. But with her lovely straight limbs, her blonde colouring, she looked like a young girl in her teens.

'Yes, he's been very kind to me,' Janet said.

'Kindness is Mark's stock in trade,' Coleen laughed. 'He's kind to everyone, a real charmer. But don't lose your heart and take him seriously, Miss Freeman — or may I call you Janet?'

'Please call me Janet.'

'Countless women have made a play for Mark,' Coleen went on. 'Maybe he's not the marrying type, or maybe he's never got over the little romance he and I once had. I'm afraid I let him down rather badly then.' She sighed. 'It was all a tragic mistake.'

'I'm sorry,' Janet murmured. She didn't want Coleen's confidences. Certainly she didn't want to discuss Mark with her.

'Mark and I are very close friends,' Coleen went on. 'Would I have come all the way over to Honolulu to welcome him otherwise?'

There was a tap on the door.

'Aren't you two girls ever going to be ready? I've news for both of you.'

Coleen went across the room with her graceful floating movements and opened the door. 'Sorry to have kept you waiting, Mark. What's the news?'

Mark stepped inside the suite. The sunshine caught his face, lit his brown hair. He looked more than ever handsome in that moment. Janet's heart missed a beat at the sight of him. She wished she had never had that conversation with Coleen Hausman. If Mark and she, Janet, had been alone here together, how wonderful everything would have been.

'What's the news?' Coleen asked again.

'I've just been down at the airways office. Apparently when we passed through that electric storm it did some damage to the plane. They say we'll be held up overnight. We're all to be the company's guests at the Royal Hawaiian. So you've got your wish, Coleen. I'll be here at least one night.'

'Goody! Goody!' she cried. 'That's splendid news, Mark. We'll do something specially exciting tonight. There's a *luau* — that's a native feast, you know — at a special restaurant I go to. They roast a pig in the *imu*. There's dancing afterwards and Hawaiian singing.'

Mark turned to Janet, it seemed deliberately. 'That sounds wonderful, doesn't it, Janet?'

Janet happened to catch a glimpse of Coleen's face in that moment. It was hard, almost angry looking, and suddenly she looked several years older.

''I thought you and I might go along together, Mark. But if you want to make a party of it . . . well, we'll have to find another man. Parties *à trois* never amuse me much.'

'It shouldn't be difficult to get another man,' Mark said. 'Haven't you made any friends while you've been here, Coleen?'

'No special friend,' she said, 'though I've talked to one or two fellow-tourists. I've been waiting for *you*, Mark.'

Mark laughed. 'You flatter me, Coleen. I can't imagine you without a host of escorts.'

Coleen shrugged. 'I might try telephoning one or two since you're so insistent this be a party.'

Janet said, and afterwards she never knew quite why she said it. 'A friend of Mark's was on the plane with us. He may care to join the party.'

Mark frowned suddenly. 'You don't mean Julian Gaden?'

'Julian Gaden! Was he on the plane with you?' Coleen's voice was slightly shrill. 'We don't want him, do we, Mark?'

'I thought you used to see a good deal of him at one time,' Mark commented.

'You mean Henry foisted him upon me. He was Henry's friend, but never mine.' Her voice was hard. 'No, I think I prefer to try and get one or other of the young men I've met around the hotel. I didn't think you liked Julian particularly either, Mark?'

Mark shrugged slightly. 'He's never been a buddy of mine. I don't dislike him, though I must say he has a way of pushing himself in on affairs when he's not wanted.'

'Exactly,' Coleen said. 'That may be one reason I've always disliked him, apart from the fact of him being Henry's friend. He was blind to Henry's faults; Henry could do no wrong in his eyes.'

'I've already got a room and booked a room for you, Janet. I won't be more than a few minutes changing. Will you wait here for me or in the foyer?'

'We'll go down on to the hotel's private beach,' Coleen said. 'You'll easily find us, Mark. I'll have the attendant get us some Lilos and beach umbrellas. We can bathe, dry off, and then stroll down to the Outrigger Club for a cocktail. That's the routine here. We can either lunch at the Outrigger Club or lunch in buffet style on the lawn at the hotel. The dining-room is big and impressive, but you have to dress for it.'

'I'm glad we're dining at that restaurant you spoke of,' Mark said. 'I haven't any dinner clothes with me — just a few things in my overnight bag. How are you placed, Janet?'

'I brought a few things along — this swimsuit and a cotton dress.'

'That will be all right,' Coleen said. 'There's no need to dress up for the restaurant where we're going. What luck your old plane was hit in the storm.'

'I shouldn't have thought it was altogether luck,' Mark said. 'It might have been a nasty accident.'

Janet remembered the terror she had felt during the storm. A little shiver went through her. She remembered, too, how she had looked across the aisle and Julian's grin and friendly gesture seemed to renew her confidence. She had been through periods of disliking him, but at that moment she had felt he was her friend. For some reason she had felt confidence in him. Was that why she had suggested that he join their party tonight?

# 7

Coleen and Janet walked through the hotel, passed the glassed-in bar at one side of the garden, out on to the beach, where the beach attendant, a native Hawaiian, a splendid specimen of manhood, brought them Lilos and a sun umbrella. It was a fascinating scene. The beach was crowded with tourists and residents; there was every shade of sun tan; the costumes were a riot of colour. The surf rolled magnificently into the beach and it was exciting watching the outrigger boats hurl into shore on the crest of a wave.

'We must go out in one of the outriggers. It's quite an experience,' Coleen said. 'As soon as Mark joins us we'll go in for a dip.'

As she spoke she waved to various couples lying on the sand. Obviously they were friends she had made during the short period of her stay here.

Mark joined them presently. Janet had seen him before in bathing trunks, but that had been in the twilight hour. In the bright sunshine his lightly tanned body glowed, his brown hair had a fairish tinge to it.

The water was unbelievably warm. She was used to the surf, after bathing at the Sydney beaches. Coleen stuck very close to Mark. Most of the time she had her hand upon his shoulder. It was a singularly possessive gesture as though she were telling the whole world she owned this man. Janet felt heartsick and discouraged. She was in love with Mark. but how could she fight against this woman who had made it fairly obvious to her in the *lanai* suite that Mark was hers?

She was swimming along by herself when she felt a hand clutch her arm. 'Hello there,' Julian Gaden's voice said. 'Don't tell me they've left you on your lonesome?'

'I just thought I'd swim along the

beach.' Her voice was cool.

'Mind if I join you? You've heard the news, of course? That storm we passed through was pretty severe. They probably want to give the plane a thorough overhauling. But it's pleasant to stay here the night, especially as we're to be the airways' guests at the Royal Hawaiian. I've been in Honolulu before, but I've never been able to rate the Royal Hawaiian.'

She was surprised. From the way he travelled about, the friends he knew, she had imagined him a rich young man. But from his remark she gathered he wasn't so rich. Then just what did he do for a living?

'Let's go up to the Outrigger Club and have a cool drink,' he suggested presently. 'I changed there. I hadn't as yet learnt we were to be guests at the Royal Hawaiian.'

They left the surf together and walked up the beach to the Outrigger Club. The attractive balcony was already crowded with people having pre-luncheon drinks.

'What'll yours be?' he asked. 'A lime squash? Or would you like something stronger?'

'A lime squash,' she said. 'I can't stay long. The others will be wondering what has become of me.'

'You mean Mark will be wondering. Coleen wouldn't give a damn.'

'You don't like her, do you?'

'No, I hate her guts. She tired of Henry almost as soon as she married him. If he did drink — which I very much doubt — she drove him to it. Poor goof, he was crazy about her. 'Other women in his life.' I never heard such nonsense.'

He signalled to the waiter and ordered a rum punch for himself and a lime squash for her.

The waiter brought the drinks almost immediately. He signed for them. 'I left my wallet in the locker,' he explained.

'Tell me,' he asked as he leant across the table towards her, 'Have you fallen for Mark Dexter?'

She felt herself flush vividly. She felt the flush had given her away. She stammered, 'I like him very much.'

Julian nodded slowly, the untidy lock of dark hair fell across his brow. He pushed it back with an impatient finger. 'That means you're pretty struck on him, I take it. I thought you were, the first time I met you. Mark's a decent chap, a bit of a stuffed shirt in some ways, but for all that I like him. If you like him as much as I think you do, you will try and get him away from Coleen Hausman. She's dynamite for men — but deadly dynamite.' He added in the pause, 'I'll be your friend in this, if you want me as a friend, Janet.'

'But why should you bother about me at all?' she said. 'It's very kind of you to offer your friendship.'

'I offered it that first night in Sydney, if you remember, when I warned you.'

She pulled her slight attractive body straighter. 'I'm still glad I came, despite Coleen Hausman. I don't think Mark is really in love with her any longer.'

'But she's out to get him,' Julian said. 'Mark is too nice; I should say he was fairly weak where women are concerned. Coleen has plenty of character. Besides, she knows just what she wants. What are you doing tonight, by the way?'

'We're going to a restaurant which is holding a *luau*, which I gather is a sort of native feast, when they roast a whole pig under the earth in an oven they call an *imu*.'

'I've seen it before. It's quite a sight when the earth is opened, the stones removed and the pig covered in ti-leaves is dug out of the earth. It's a moment for rejoicing. Would you come with me, Janet?'

'I promised the others I would go with them.'

He made a wry grimace. 'You couldn't get me included in the party?'

'I tried,' she admitted, 'but apparently Mrs. Hausman has other friends around the hotel.'

'You mean she turned me down? But

it was nice of you to try. I'll be sticking around, anyhow. Maybe you'll spare a dance or two for me?'

She nodded. She had disliked him in the past, but ever since that incident in the plane she had found herself liking him. She liked him even more now that he had promised to help her get Mark disentangled from Coleen.

'I must go,' she said.

He rose to his feet. 'I'll walk up the beach with you.'

But as it happened, there was no need to walk along the beach; they encountered Mark and Coleen sitting at the corner table drinking an iced punch which was served in a scooped-out pineapple, a feature of the island and most attractive looking.

Mark rose to his feet. 'We wondered where you'd got to, Janet.'

'I met Julian in the surf. We came up here for a cool drink.'

Mark said, 'Won't you join us?'

Coleen hadn't spoken a word. She was looking at Julian with hard, angry eyes. Her face seemed slightly paler, and it had hardened, too. She no longer looked a girl in that moment; she looked twenty-six or more.

'We'll be glad to join you, won't we, Janet? I can always use another drink.' And then for the first time he turned and addressed Coleen:

'Hello, Coleen. Aren't we speaking any longer?'

'If you wish,' she murmured. Her voice was tight and strained.

'You've never forgiven me for being one of Henry's best friends, have you?' he said as they sat down at the table.

'Poor Henry,' she said. 'Need we mention him?'

'What's this story you've been putting around about Henry drinking and going in for other dames?' he accused her bluntly.

She threw up her head and looked defiant. 'Well, it was true.'

'I knew him pretty well,' Julian said. 'As far as I know, he never drank to excess, nor did he look at other women.

He looked only at you, Coleen. It's a pity you couldn't find it in yourself to return his love.'

'He didn't love me,' she snapped back at him, 'or he wouldn't have behaved the way he did out in Hollywood. You weren't out in Hollywood with us, Julian, when Henry was working on that script for Paramount. You don't know what happened to him out there. Besides, you never liked me; you've always been prejudiced in Henry's favour.'

'I was his friend. I am still his friend,' Julian said simply.

'But he's dead.' There was a note of hysteria in her voice. 'How can you be the friend of a man who is dead?'

'I can be a friend to a man who is dead,' he said very quietly. 'At least I can save his reputation from being smeared.'

All through this conversation Mark was looking increasingly embarrassed. He made several interjections as though he were trying to break it up, but both

Coleen and Julian were too intent on what they were saying. For a moment the others might not have existed for them.

'Try one of these pineapple punches,' Mark suggested to Janet. 'They're delicious and not too strong.'

'Very well.' She gave a small laugh. 'I'm game to try anything once.'

They were still talking in undertones.

'We looked everywhere for you on the beach,' he said. 'I was worried, Janet.'

Her heart beat quicker. A flush of pleasure stained her cheeks. 'Were you really worried, Mark?'

'I was,' he said. 'It's my responsibility to see you reach New York safely.'

But would his responsibility end there, she wondered? She felt slightly bleak.

Janet had the pineapple drink. It was ice-cold and delicious. The pineapple was scooped out and the punch mixed with pineapple juice was poured inside. Mark tried to make the conversation general, but Coleen was in a peevish mood.

'I don't think we'll lunch here after all,' she said. 'It's too crowded today.'

Mark laughed. 'Yes, I agree. And since the airways is paying for all our meals at the Royal Hawaiian, we may as well lunch there, especially as we are going out to the *luau* to-night.'

'I'm thinking of going, too,' Julian said. He grinned across at Coleen with a touch of malice. 'You wouldn't include me in the party, I suppose?'

'I'm sorry,' she said stiffly. 'I've already asked another friend of mine who's staying at the hotel. When you've finished your drink, Janet, we'll be getting back to the Royal Hawaiian.'

Janet finished her drink as quickly as she could. The atmosphere at the table was distinctly embarrassing, even electric. It was obvious these two hated each other, and both of them could hate pretty effectively. Janet found herself thinking she wouldn't like to come up against either one of them.

And yet if she was to come to mean anything to Mark, how could she avoid one day a showdown with Coleen Hausman?

They changed up in Coleen's suite before going down to the buffet luncheon at the Royal Hawaiian. Janet had only one dress in her overnight bag. It was a pretty dress of glazed cotton with a gold and green motif that went excellently with her hair and colouring. It was one of her extravagances which she had bought just before she left Sydney.

Coleen wore a strapless sunsuit. It was the pale gold of her skin and hair. She wore diamond studs in her ears. She pinned an orchid into her hair and put on again the lei of orchids she had been wearing when she met their plane.

Janet also put on her lei of sweet-smelling ginger flowers. Mark had already discarded his, but he wore white trousers cut fashionably tight and a multicoloured sunshirt.

The buffet luncheon had already

begun. It was served out in the garden, and the surroundings were most attractive. The women mainly wore strapless dresses such as the one Coleen was wearing, of vivid colours, with flower leis around their neck and flowers pinned into their hair. The men with their exotically coloured aloha shirts contributed to the vivid brilliance of the picture. Just across the garden the surf broke on the golden sands. It was certainly an enchanting spot.

Coleen had stopped to talk to some friends she had made in the hotel. Janet and Mark, plate in hand, wandered about the lavishly stocked buffet table. He pointed out to her the various native dishes and suggested she try them. She didn't think much of *poi*, the national dish. It tasted too much like watery potatoes. But the *Lomi* salmon was delicious.

'Don't eat the pig,' Mark suggested. 'You'll be eating that tonight.'

There was turkey, chicken and salads. She soon had her plate piled high.

Coleen had joined them by this time and the three of them sat and ate at a table in the bright warm sunshine.

'Why don't you take a tourist bus this afternoon and see something of the island?' Coleen suggested to Janet. 'There's a trip that goes to the No-na-me Waterfall and then takes you to the cliff where the Koolau Mountains drop off in a sharp plunge to the slope of Kanehoe. It's quite something to see.'

Janet glanced towards Mark, but in some embarrassment he looked away from her. 'I'm afraid I'm not available to show you the sights this afternoon, Janet. It appears Coleen has ordered a stack of clothes and wants my advice.'

'Of course I want your advice, Mark,' Coleen broke in. 'That's why I put off making my decisions until you arrived.' She turned to Janet: 'I always take a man along shopping with me. Saleswomen can be so persuasive; they'll make you buy something that's really hideous on you. I'm weak where saleswomen are concerned; I need masculine support.'

Janet wished again with all her heart that Coleen had never come here. Mark would be taking her to see the sights then. They would be together in the same blissful way they had been together in Nadi on the Fiji Islands. But there was nothing for her to do but to thank Mark for making the arrangement for her.

'The bus leaves the hotel at two-fifteen. You'll have to hurry with your lunch, Janet.'

'I want to take you over to those friends I was talking to before we started lunch, Mark,' Coleen said. 'He's a company director, quite a big shot, and his wife is very charming. I see that Leslie Henderson has joined them. He's the man I want to co-opt for our party tonight. Janet should be thrilled. He's an up-and-coming TV star. I think he's going big places.'

Janet supposed she ought to be grateful, but for the moment she had no eyes for any other man but Mark. And Mark would be with Coleen all that afternoon in the intimacy of fashionable gown houses, seeing her in one bewitching gown after another, helping her choose them. She gritted her teeth. 'Yes, I'd better hurry to catch that bus,' she said aloud.

Janet had no taste so see the sights alone and ever since their talk together that morning she had found herself liking Julian. She admired him, too, for his outspoken words to Coleen. He didn't fawn upon her as other men seemed to, even Mark. That hurt sharply.

In the foyer she stopped and asked for his room number. She hadn't much hope that he would be there, but she put through a call to him.

It just happened he was there. He had just finished his lunch. She explained about the excursion Mark had booked her on. 'I suppose you wouldn't like to come along and keep me company?'

'Sure I'll come,' he said promptly. 'I've been there before, but that doesn't stop me wanting to go again — with you, Janet. What's the great Mark doing this afternoon?'

'Helping Coleen choose some gowns.' She felt ashamed to have to admit it.

He chuckled. 'I'd say any excuse is good enough for Coleen to keep him away from you. The girl is like a bloodhound when she scents a rival. I'll be down in a jiffy and meet you in the foyer.'

# 8

Janet felt considerably heartened. She liked Julian though she couldn't imagine ever falling in love with him; he was too blunt, too outspoken. He hadn't Mark's charm and appeal. But his company was far preferable to going on a tourist bus on her own. Besides, childishly, she would like Mark to know that Julian had been her escort that afternoon. At Nadi he had seemed to resent very strongly Julian's butting in upon them.

In the light tropical suit he was wearing, Julian looked taller and leaner and more loosely put together than ever. He had brushed his black hair back, but she sensed it would soon flop over his forehead again in that untidy way.

They boarded the bus and were lucky enough to get front seats. She felt excited now at the prospect of seeing more of this wonderful island. The bus took them down the Pali Road through the Nuuana Valley. The scenery was superb, green tropical foliage, flowering shrubs and trees, large isolated bungalows with heavenly gardens. The driver acted as guide and stopped to show them the No-na-me Falls, explaining they were called that as no satisfactory name had ever been found for them.

Presently they were climbing through the mountains and at last reached the top of a gigantic cliff where the Koolu Mountain plunged down to the windy slope of Kamehoe. Janet gasped at the splendour of it. 'This must be one of the most wonderful sights of this world,' she said.

A fierce wind was blowing. The driver threw coins into the wind only to have them hurtled back at him again.

'Some people come here to commit suicide,' he said, 'but they're blown right back. Funny, eh?' — and he giggled.

Their next stop was Kaneohe Bay, where the Marine Coral Gardens are. They went out in a glass-bottomed boat; the water was crystal clear and they could gaze down at the fantastic coral world. The coral was fashioned in every shape and size, fantastically lovely; brightly-coloured fish swam amongst the dainty coral structures.

Julian pointed out to her several fishes — the indigo bird fish, some sunshine-coloured lauwilis. Her small pretty face gazed down upon all these wonders with delight and astonishment. 'I never thought anything could be so beautiful,' she said.

'You're not sorry, then, you came on this outing?'

'Not in the least. If I'd stayed behind in the hotel, I never would have seen half of these wonders. I would have known nothing of Honolulu but the Royal Hawaiian Hotel and Waikiki Beach.'

'You're glad I came along with you?'

She smiled that lovely warm smile of

hers, when her whole face lit up. She reached across and touched his hand in gratitude. 'Very glad, Julian. Thank you.'

'I'm thanking you for giving me the opportunity. I like to be with you, Janet. You didn't like me very much at first, did you, because I tried to warn you against coming over to the States. I didn't expect at the time that you'd take much notice of me. But I liked you. I felt I had to warn you.'

'If Mark was in love with Coleen, surely he would have married her long ago,' she said.

'I wouldn't think Mark was all that much in love with her,' he said. 'But because they were playmates in their youth, he feels protective towards her.'

She sighed. 'I hope that is the truth. You wouldn't be just saying that to keep my spirits up?'

He shook his head. 'I'm not tactful, Janet. I'm often accused of being too outspoken. Did you think me too outspoken this morning?'

'It was embarrassing, to say the least of it.'

'I know.' His face turned hard and grim. 'But it's difficult for me to keep my temper when I see Coleen the centre of attention and I know how deeply she made Henry suffer. But I'm sorry if I embarrassed you and Mark. I'll try to keep my temper in future.'

He had been looking down into the marine underground. The lock of hair had fallen again untidily across his brow. She had a sudden impulse to push it back for him. She couldn't understand the impulse. She had outgrown her dislike for him, but that was all.

He grinned across at her. 'I need a haircut,' he said. 'Maybe I should have a crew-cut, and then I'd have no trouble with that dashed lock of hair. I tried it once, but I looked something fearful.'

She laughed. 'No, I don't think a crew-cut would suit you.'

After that they drove through fields

of pineapples being harvested. Pineapples are one of the chief exports of Hawaii. The bus stopped a moment so that they could watch the huge machines scything the pineapples off, and then dropping them neatly into the waiting trucks. 'Swarms of Hawaiians used to do it by hand in the old days,' Julian told her. 'But this is the mechanical age. It's a pity, because despite the tourist boom there's still a good deal of unemployment amongst the native Hawaiians.'

When they returned to the hotel, Julian invited her out to the bar to have a cocktail.

'I must go and tidy up first,' she said. 'I haven't even seen my room.'

He grinned. 'It won't be a *lanai* suite like Coleen Hausman has. The airways may put us up buckshee, but they don't run to *lanai* suites.'

The room was small but very nice. It was at the side of the hotel and looked out on to a garden of scarlet bougainvillea and the multicoloured hibiscus.

There were also exotic orchids, and she saw at closer range the colourful, spectacular bird-of-paradise flower.

I'd love to stay here for days, she thought, if only Coleen Hausman were somewhere else!

She wished she'd brought another dress to change into but it was by the sheerest fluke she had included in her overnight bag this printed glazed floral dress. She hoped that at the *luau* there would be other women in cotton dresses, that she wouldn't be conspicuous.

The bar was in the garden and adjoined the hotel. It was an attractive glassed-in pavilion and it opened out on to a tiled patio that fronted the beach. She drank another of the pineapple punches and Julian joined her. She had been feeling rather tired after the long day and sleepless night, but the drink refreshed her.

Julian raised one black untidy eyebrow. 'Still glad you asked me to come along this afternoon?'

She nodded. 'Very glad.'

'In Sydney you disliked me,' he said. 'Am I still in disfavour?'

She smiled and impulsively stretched out a hand to him. 'You're forgiven though I only hope all the evils you prophesied won't come true.'

He held her hand, squeezing it closely. 'I hope so, too, Janet. But you do know now you can look upon me as a friend in anything.'

'Well, so this is where you are!'

They hadn't seen Mark approaching them. He stood beside the table, glaring down at them. Janet was terribly conscious that Julian was still holding her hand. She knew that Mark was aware of it. He didn't look in the least pleased.

Julian dropped her hand and grinned. 'Sit down and join us in a drink, Mark.'

'I'm afraid I haven't time,' Mark said. His voice was stiff. 'Coleen and Mr. Henderson are waiting in the foyer. It's time we started for the *luau*. I've been looking for you everywhere, Janet.' He had never spoken to her so curtly before.

She felt a mist of tears behind her eyes.

'I'll come now, Mark. Will you excuse me, Julian?'

'Since you must go, you must, I suppose,' he said. 'But I'm thinking of taking in that same *luau* tonight. I'll see you there.'

'I've been calling and calling your room,' Mark said as they left the bar together. 'Did you enjoy the trip this afternoon? I'm glad you went.'

She didn't tell him that Julian had gone with her. She hoped he wouldn't know. He seemed cross enough that he had found them drinking together at the bar. But he had been out all afternoon with Coleen Hausman. What did he expect of her?

She felt distinctly embarrassed when she joined the small party in the foyer. Coleen was elaborately dressed in a short evening gown of lace and taffeta. It was the same blue as her eyes. She also wore a diamond necklace, the diamonds winking in the lights, and there were diamonds in her ears. Knowing that Janet had no change of clothes, it would have been kinder of her to dress more simply.

She was introduced to Leslie Henderson, a tallish young man with very blond hair, blue-grey eyes and a frank boyish smile that had an intimate quality about it. You felt whenever he smiled he was especially smiling at you; you were the one person in the whole world who counted.

The restaurant was a white painted building on the outskirts of the town, with a wide courtyard. Tourists and Hawaiians were arriving in great numbers. The aristocratic-looking Hawaiian women looked marvellous in their magnificently embroidered holokulas, a loose garment with a train. Janet decided she was probably the most modestly dressed girl in the whole room.

The tables were placed round a

dance-floor. There was a stage at one end of the room where there would be music for dancing, and the Hawaiian serenaders would sing. 'There will be hula dancing as well,' Coleen told her. 'Personally I'm not a great enthusiast for hula dancing — wriggling brown bodies in their grass skirts. You get too much of it here. It bores me.'

'I believe lots of tourists take lessons in the art of hula dancing when they're over here,' Leslie Henderson remarked. 'But I can't see them doing it in their native home towns in the States.' He laughed. He had a very pleasing laugh. His was altogether a very pleasing personality. Janet could understand that he had already gone far as a compère on TV. He was still very young; he would probably go a great deal further.

He was very pleasant to her, but it was obvious that he was chiefly attracted to Coleen. His eyes rarely left her, and she was certainly glittering and dazzling enough that night to hold any man's attention. She monopolised the conversation, addressing first Mark, then Leslie Henderson, ignoring Janet. Janet might not have been there.

On several occasions Mark tried to bring Janet into the conversation, but Coleen always neatly side-tracked him, bringing the conversation back to herself.

Cocktails and canapés were served; everything apparently was included in the price of the evening's entertainment.

The band was playing but as yet no one was dancing; everyone waited for the moment when they would be called out into the courtyard to see the roasted pig dug up out of its earthy oven. Presently the head waiter suggested that the hour was ripe.

It was quite a ceremony. There was a full moon that night, and the flowering shrubs in the gardens made the atmosphere heady with perfume. First a Hawaiian, naked to the waist and magnificently shaped, shovelled earth from on top of the *imu*. After that, heavy stones were taken off, and finally they peered down the hole and saw the pig lying on hot stones, wrapped in ti-leaves.

'It's the most perfect way in this whole world I know of cooking a pig,' Mark observed. 'Just wait until you've tasted it, Janet.'

He had moved beside her. At some little distance away Leslie Henderson was talking to Coleen, exerting all his charm upon her.

'You didn't mind my leaving you this afternoon, Janet?' Mark asked quietly. 'Coleen at heart is such a child. She depends upon a man; she always has. I'm afraid since her husband's tragic death, she has come to depend upon me. I know she likes me and tries to monopolise me — that's her way. Don't let it worry you, please, Janet.' His voice was low and urgent.

'I'll try not to let it worry me,' she said. 'But it isn't always easy, Mark.'

'I know. We've been very close for the past weeks, haven't we Janet? Of course

I was pleased to see Coleen, but I almost wish she hadn't come. Damn it, I wanted to be the one to show you Hawaii — just you and I.'

'I wanted that, too, Mark.'

'You did?' His voice was boyish, eager. 'Do you feel the same towards me as I feel towards you, Janet?'

'I feel a strong attraction, anyhow. I felt it the first moment I met you in Alvin Harvey's office.'

'I hope we're going to see quite a lot of each other in New York; and that's quite apart from office hours.'

Her small, pretty face was flushed with pleasure. Her bright hazel eyes shone. But before she could make any reply, Coleen and Leslie Henderson had joined them.

'What have you two been whispering about?' Coleen asked. 'About those manuscripts Janet is going to edit for you?'

Mark stiffened; he looked annoyed. 'This is scarcely the place to talk business.'

'No,' Coleen agreed, and made a gamin-like grin that had malice in it. 'I didn't think it was business, somehow. Well, we've seen the pig taken out of the *imu*. Let's all go inside and dance until they've cut up the pig and are ready to serve it to us.'

The Hawaiian Serenaders had been engaged for the evening and were singing haunting Hawaiians songs on the raised dais:

'A lei of love I give to you
To think of me when you are blue.
Wherever you may be on land or sea,
For you a lei to remember me.'

'Most Hawaiian songs are shockingly sentimental,' Coleen laughed. 'They seem to express a great sense of sadness, and yet from what I've seen of the Hawaiian people, they are proud but gay.'

Presently they started on another number:

'There's perfume in a million flowers,
Clinging to the heart of old Hawaii;
There's a rainbow following the showers,
Bring me part of old Hawaii.
There's a silver moon, a symphony of stars,
There's a hula tune and a hum of soft guitars;
There's a trade wind singing in the heavens,
Singing me a song of old Hawaii.'

Coleen laid a hand on Mark's arm in that same possessive way as she had laid it on his shoulder when they were swimming together in the surf. 'Let's dance, Mark,' she said softly.

Leslie Henderson turned to Janet: 'Would you care to dance, Miss Freeman?'

She said, 'I've love to,' though she knew she'd rather be dancing with Mark to these haunting Hawaiian melodies. But surely he would ask her for the next dance? That conversation they had had out in the garden of the restaurant while the pig was being dug up from the *imu* had given her new hope.

'I understand you're a very popular person on TV,' she said to Leslie Henderson.

'You flatter me,' he said, giving her his nice intimate smile that made her feel she was the only girl worth noticing on the dance-floor. 'I've made some start anyhow, but I'm far from the famous personality I want to be yet. Before I started on TV I was in films in Hollywood. That's where I met Coleen Hausman.'

She was sufficiently curious to ask, 'Did you know her husband, too?'

'Of course,' he said. 'Henry Hausman was a great guy. He worked on the script for one of the films I was making.'

'I heard he drank?' she added quickly. 'But one hears so many lies about people.'

'If anyone said Henry Hausman drank to excess, that is a downright lie,' Leslie answered emphatically. 'He wouldn't touch a drink while he was working, and in the evening — and I saw them fairly frequently in the evenings — his drinking was very moderate.'

'It must have been an awful car smash he was involved in.'

'I can't understand it,' Leslie said. 'Henry was the best of drivers. But apparently suddenly he lost control. My private opinion is that he had a heart attack or something.'

So here was a second report on Henry Hausman, denying everything which Coleen had told Mark.

'This will be your first visit to New York?' he suggested.

She nodded. 'Yes. I've always longed to go, but until recently I never had the opportunity.'

'You must come and let me show you round our TV studios. After that we'll lunch together.'

'It's very kind of you,' Janet said. 'Your time must be fully occupied in New York.'

He smiled down at her again in that intimate way. 'One always has time to spare for a pretty girl. And if I may say so, you are very pretty, Miss Freeman.'

She sensed that complimenting women was his stock in trade. All the same his compliment pleased her; she no longer felt so much out of things in the printed dress she was wearing.

When they returned to the table the famous pig was being served. It was delicious. Janet had never tasted anything so succulent. The trimmings were exciting too, and Mark ordered champagne to go with it. They made conventional conversation throughout the meal. The pig was followed by a delightful sweet of crushed pineapple, strawberries, nuts and cream.

The room was crowded. As well as the Hawaiian women in their holokulas there were plenty of American tourists, the women beautifully gowned, most of them wearing jewels. The men looked very smart in their white dinner jackets.

After dinner Mark asked her to dance. She had danced with him before in Sydney, but she felt the same thrill now as he put his arms about her and they started dancing. He danced in a loose, easy style; their steps fitted perfectly.

'Are you enjoying it, Janet?'

'Very much.' But that was half a lie. She would have enjoyed herself so much more if Coleen Hausman had not been present.

'I want to try and repay you for all the good times you gave me in Sydney. You'll let me take you about in New York, won't you?'

She laughed. 'Of course. I'll be thrilled.'

'I'll explore New York again through your eyes. Just the two of us, Janet. You want that, don't you?'

She said, 'Yes, I want that, Mark.'

His hold upon her waist tightened. He drew her closer.

'I'm always glad to see Coleen, of course,' he said presently.

'She's such a very old friend. But I wish she hadn't come all the way from New York to meet me here. It makes me feel responsible for her. You see that, don't you, Janet?' His voice was anxious.

'Yes, I see that,' she agreed. 'But I wish we were alone together like we were in Fiji, Mark.'

'You mean until Julian butted in upon us. That man's becoming a dashed nuisance. Why did you go out to the bar and have a drink with him tonight, Janet?' His voice almost accused her.

'He invited me. I thought you were engaged with Coleen.'

'I can't like that fellow,' he said morosely. 'Look how rude he was to Coleen while we were having drinks at the Outrigger Club today. Surely if anyone knew her own husband, she should know him. But he almost implied that she was lying.'

'Do you think she was very much in love with her husband, Mark?'

He hesitated. 'Maybe she wasn't, but after she'd told me what he was like, who could blame her? She eloped with him on a silly infatuation. She's always doing impulsive things — like coming over here to meet me. She's a child in so many ways. Sometimes I think she's never grown up.'

But a greedy child, a wilful child, Janet thought.

The music ceased and they returned to their table. The band-leader announced the band would play 'The Cockeyed Mayor of Kaunakakai.'

'This is better,' Coleen said. 'This is fun.'

A member of the band was wearing a battered top-hat at a comical angle. He was singing:

'He wore a malo and a coconut hat,
The one for this and the other for that,

All the people shouted as he went by,
He was the cockeyed mayor of Kaunakakai.'

Everyone laughed and applauded as though the comical song had lifted their spirits. When the next dance started, Janet saw Julian pushing his way through the dancers to their table.

'Hello, everyone!' He wore that lopsided grin. 'May I have this dance, Janet?'

Coleen said acidly, 'We are an even party as you must see, Julian.'

He ignored her. 'You won't refuse me this one dance, Janet?'

'No. I'll be glad to dance with you, Julian.' She spoke with defiance. She looked round at the others. 'Will you excuse me, please?'

Mark nodded curtly. He was scowling. Only Leslie smiled at her.

'I don't seem too popular with your dinner companions,' Julian remarked as they started dancing. He was smiling, but in rather a grim way. 'I guess Coleen has it in for me for what I said at the Outrigger Club. Maybe I shouldn't have spoken so openly, but there's something about that woman that brings out the worst in me. What do you think of her, Janet?'

'I can't say I like her,' Janet said. 'I should think she's supremely selfish.'

'And determined,' Julian added. 'By the way, I was browsing through the New York papers which have just been flown in. I came across a paragraph which I thought might interest you. I want to show it to you. Let's step outside. There are lights in the garden.'

The patio was lighted and there were fairy-lights stretched in the garden. He pulled out his wallet and took from it a clipping: 'This was in one of the gossip columns,' he said —

> 'Why has a rich, glamorous young widow, a leader of Café Society, suddenly flown out to Honolulu? It couldn't be to meet a certain

handsome publisher, who is just returning from Down Under? Do I hear the faint note of wedding bells?

'She must have given that notice to the gossip-column writer herself,' he said. 'I told you, Janet, she was dynamite. Are you still as much in love with Mark?'

She nodded, 'Yes.'

'I wish you weren't.' He sighed. 'But I'll hold by my promise to be your friend. Let's walk further down into the garden, Janet. There's such a mob on the dance-floor. Besides, as I needn't tell you, I'm not a very good dancer.'

His style was too jerky. He was difficult to follow. He didn't dance smoothly and easily as Mark did.

It was a lovely garden. The air was heady with the scent of flowers. A shrubbery at one end cut them off from the restaurant, but the strains of the plaintive music followed them out.

Julian stopped and put his hand on her arm. 'I asked you to kiss me once before, Janet. Would you kiss me now — even though it's just a friendly kiss?' There was humility in his voice which surprised her. His voice was usually hard and arrogant.

He had been so kind to her today she didn't like to refuse him. 'Just one kiss,' she murmured.

She was surprised at the gentleness with which he drew her into his arms. His kiss fell tenderly on her lips and then became more insistent. At one time, during the period she had disliked him, she had thought his kisses would revolt her. But they didn't revolt her, although they didn't thrill her as Mark's kisses that night at Nadi had thrilled her.

He let her go presently and said, 'Thank you, Janet. Some day, perhaps, I'll kiss you again. You may even respond. I'm not giving up hope. I suppose I've kept you out here long enough. Do you want to go back and join your table?'

Strangely she felt she would rather

stay out in the garden with him for a little while. Despite Leslie Henderson's charm, the atmosphere at the table wasn't altogether pleasant. There was an undercurrent between Mark and Coleen she didn't understand. Surely Coleen had got her way with him; she had had him to herself all that afternoon. She wondered if Mark had seen that notice in the gossip column about the wedding bells? Coleen might be trying to drive Mark into marriage. But Janet had a feeling that Mark wasn't a man to be driven easily. He would make his own decisions. He would resent any decision — even one coming from Coleen, whom he obviously liked — being forced upon him.

Mark and she danced once again before the evening ended. He looked displeased with her and her heart felt heavy.

'You were out a deuce of a time with that Gaden fellow,' he accused her. 'Just what were you doing?'

'We were wandering in the garden.

It's noisy and hot in here, Mark. It was lovely out there.'

'I'd like to take you out into the garden myself,' he said. 'But Coleen would notice.'

She looked directly up at him. 'Are you afraid of her, Mark?'

He hesitated. 'I don't want to upset her, anyhow. As I said, it was decent of her to fly out here to meet me. Besides, if she's upset she's apt to get into rather childish rages. You and I will have plenty of time to be together in New York, Janet,' and he added in a lower voice, 'my dear.'

She wished it had been 'my darling,' the way he had said it that night in Nadi. Obviously something had upset Coleen and it worried him. She told herself she must bide her time, she must wait. But when you are so much in love with anyone as she was with Mark, it was difficult to wait.

There was hula dancing before the evening was over. A group of native girls in grass skirts with leis about their necks and flowers in their hair, did some expert hula dancing. Their lithe brown bodies twisted and swayed. They kept up to an insistent beat of music with their bare brown feet. Janet had seen the hula danced on the stage, but this was something different — out of this world. And in the atmosphere it was quite perfect.

It was Mark who suggested they should be getting back. 'We have to be at the airport early in the morning,' he said.

Coleen caught his arm, her voice pleaded with him. 'Why not stay a few days longer, Mark? Send Janet on. After I've come out all this way to meet you, I think you owe it to me.'

But Mark was very firm. 'Sorry, Coleen, my dear, business is piling up in the office. Besides, I want to be there to introduce Janet around to all the other members of the staff and fix what work she's going to do.'

Coleen pouted, but prettily. 'You are a meanie, Mark. What am I going to do here on my lonesome? I've booked for another week.'

'I'll try and see you're not bored, Coleen,' Leslie Henderson said, with his famous smile. 'There are seaplane trips to the other islands. We might go on a voyage of exploration.'

'Yes, that would be nice.' But she spoke flatly. Her blue eyes as she looked across at Mark were still hard and angry.

She gave a small laugh and said, 'You should be chasing *me*, Mark. It seems I'm always chasing *you*. I may not stay a whole week here; I may be back in New York any day.'

'I'm always delighted to see you, Coleen,' Mark said, but he spoke stiffly.

Janet sensed he hadn't liked that remark about her chasing him. Mark, as she had thought before, would always want to make his own decisions.

# 9

The green coral islands with their purple hills faded into nothingness as they flew higher into the air. Soon there were only clouds about them and the sparkling blue of the sky. It was wonderful to feel that Mark and she were alone again, without Coleen's clinging presence. She had come down to the airstrip to see them off, wearing a lei of jasmine and orchids and jasmine flowers in her hair. She threw a lei of ginger flowers about Mark's shoulder, singing softly:

'A lei of flowers I give to you,
To think of me when you are blue.'

'Thanks a lot, Coleen,' Mark said. 'But I feel an awful fool decked out like this.'

'But it's the custom here, honey,' she

smiled. 'Besides, I do want you to think of me when you're away. She thrust her arm through his, clinging to him. 'You will, won't you, Mark? You're not annoyed with me for coming over to meet you in Honolulu?'

'I'm immensely flattered, of course. I've enjoyed every moment of my stay here.'

'Thank you, darling.' She kissed Mark behind the ear. Coleen was the most uninhibited of people.

Janet was conscious that Julian was watching this little scene, a faintly sardonic smile upon his face. 'What, no lei for me, Coleen?' His voice was malicious, mocking.

'I only give leis to those whom I consider my friends,' she said coldly. But she hadn't brought Janet a lei either.

'Be seeing you soon, darling,' she said to Mark. 'Leslie is amusing enough, but from my own experience, all TV commentators are full of conceit.'

'He seemed a very pleasant young man,' Mark said.

Coleen gave an impish grin back at him. 'I hoped you'd be jealous, darling.'

But now Mark and Janet were alone, or as much alone as you can be in a crowded plane. She liked Julian; she now regarded him as her friend; but she wished he hadn't been sitting so close to them just across the aisle. It seemed to spoil the sense of intimacy she wanted to establish between Mark and herself.

The day was dying in golden colours when they finally reached San Francisco. They had a brief few hours to spare before catching the plane to New York. It was still daylight as they circled to touch down at the airport. From this height San Francisco looked as though it had been built at an angle of forty-five degrees. The streets with their cable cars seemed to plunge straight down from the hills.

'We must ride in a cable car,' Mark said. 'It's absolutely the thing to do in San Francisco. We'll dine at Fisherman's Wharf and then go up and see the town at night from the roof of the Mark Hopkins Hotel. San Francisco is one of the most fascinating cities in the States. I wish we had more time to spend here.'

Jane wished it too. It would be glorious to be seeing this fascinating city alone with Mark. Besides, the nearer she drew to New York the more she had to admit to a sense of nervousness. Her mother had not sounded very welcoming in her cabled reply. What would happen once they met again in the ridiculous situation of two sisters? Would her mother be anything like how she remembered her — nut-brown-haired, a few grey hairs showing, dark almond-shaped eyes? In her youth she had been considered very beautiful. How would they greet each other in this new relationship her mother had insisted upon? Would Tim have changed much from the slim, good-looking young man he had been with the waving brown hair and amber flecks in his eyes? Would he welcome her or resent her presence? Was it because of Tim her mother had never invited her over and had replied unenthusiastically to her cable telling her that she was coming?

But the excitement of travelling around San Francisco with Mark put these thoughts out of her mind. The ride in the cable car down almost cliff-like streets was exciting. The drive through Chinatown with its streets crammed with shops selling Chinese wares, its restaurants, the Chinese signs suspended from them, was a thrill. Mark held her arm closely and seemed to enjoy it all as much as she did. The sun was setting as they passed the two famous bridges, the Golden Gate and the Bay Bridge.

The restaurant at Fisherman's Wharf was a delightful place, nautical in decoration. They ate sea-food, oysters, and delicious grilled lobsters.

'I feel as though I'm on a roller coaster,' Janet laughed across to Mark. 'So much to see, so much to take in in a short space of time.'

'I've been in San Francisco often,' Mark said. 'But I've never enjoyed it as much as I have these past few hours here with you Janet. Did I tell you you were very sweet?' He caught both her hands and held them under the table. His dark grey eyes looked directly across into her face. 'You're lovely,' he said. 'So fresh and young. You make me feel a boy again.'

'You're not so very old,' she laughed.

'I'm twenty-eight and should know better than to be holding hands with a girl as young as you, Janet. I wish we could spend the night here and visit Chinatown, but alas, there's so much work waiting for me in New York. I'm going to keep you pretty busy, Janet. You won't mind?'

'That's what I've come over for, to do a lot of hard work for you.'

He smiled. 'And to play with me sometimes, I hope. I've plenty of friends, but sometimes I'm lonely, Janet. You and I will creep away from the office and go out somewhere and dine; somewhere where I'm not liable to run into any of my friends. Just you and I together. Will you like that?'

She smiled back at him, her eyes were misty. 'I shall like that more than anything in this world.'

'You're a wonderful girl,' he said. 'So understanding. You even seem to understand about Coleen and me.'

Her heart missed a beat. 'Is there anything special to understand, Mark?'

'Only that she's one of my dearest friends and seems to have a proprietary interest in me. Sometimes it can be a bit embarrassing. But that's Coleen's line — utter frankness. At one time I was in love with her. But of course that's all in the past.'

She looked across at him steadily. She had to know. '*Is* it in the past, Mark?'

'As far as I'm concerned, it is.' He shrugged. 'I still like her very much and enjoy her company. I'd do a great deal for her — almost anything. If we're going to be the sort of friends I hope we're going to be, Janet, you must understand about Coleen and me. As I told you once, we were practically brought up together.'

'And then you fell in love,' she said.

He nodded. 'At least I fell in love with her. She can't have loved me very much, because in the midst of our affair she suddenly eloped with Henry Hausman. I was pretty bitter about it at the time, but after she was widowed and came back to New York we resumed our old relationship. She's so damned attractive, I can't think why she has never married again.'

Janet thought she knew the answer to that. She didn't like the answer.

Shortly they were airborne once again on the final lap of their journey to New York. She had spoken to Julian briefly. While Mark was out in the observation lounge he came over for a minute and asked her what she thought of San Francisco.

'I loved every minute I spent there.'

He grinned a little sourly. 'That's because you had Mark all to yourself. Incidentally, I saw you go into the Fisherman's Wharf Restaurant. I nearly joined you, but I didn't.' He lowered his voice and added, 'I promised I'd help you out as much as I could, Janet.'

She smiled and said, 'Thank you.' And then Mark was back.

'That fellow Julian Gaden never leaves you alone for a moment, does he?' he said in an undertone. 'Are you sure you're not encouraging him, Janet?'

'No. I'm not,' she said, but she felt guilty. She had telephoned Julian that day in Honolulu, asking him to go on the tourist bus with her. She wasn't altogether sorry; it had been a very pleasant afternoon. But she hoped Mark would never find it out.

Shortly after take-off the lights were lowered and the passengers settled down to sleep. Janet had never felt less like sleep. Now that the trip was nearing its end she was all tension.

Tomorrow she would actually see her mother again after a lapse of eleven years. How would they act towards each other? She couldn't know. She wished she could confide in Mark, but Mark had a conventional attitude towards life. He wouldn't understand. It was difficult even for her to understand, this insistence of her mother's that she be regarded as her sister.

Oddly, she thought she could more easily have confided in Julian. But it was safer to confide in no one. It was such a ridiculous situation, anyhow. She tugged at the rug, half turned aside from Mark towards the window, determined if possible to get some sleep.

# 10

They touched down at Idlewild Airport shortly before noon. While they were going through Customs and Immigration she met Julian for a moment briefly.

'You will be staying at the Beekman Towers Hotel, won't you? I'll contact you there.'

'I may be staying with my sister.' It was still hard to get those last words out.

'I told you I knew Tim Warren, didn't I? And your sister, the famous Madame June. But if you want my advice, which you don't always appreciate, I'd stay at the Beekman Towers Hotel. There is nothing like being independent.'

'I gather Mark has already arranged for a room for me at the Beekman Towers Hotel. I'll go there first, anyhow.'

She had wondered whether her mother would meet the plane. But with the delay in Honolulu it seemed unlikely she should do so. But as they emerged from the Customs and Immigration Offices, a tall, well-set-up man in his middle thirties came towards them.

It had been eleven years since she had last seen Tim Warren. She had been a child, but she recognised him instantly. He still looked the young and handsome man she remembered. She had always known he was a good deal younger than her mother, but he didn't seem to have aged at all. Once she had hated this man more than she had ever hated anyone, for taking her mother from her, for bringing a great sadness into her father's life. His wife's desertion had been a blow from which the professor had never really recovered. She told herself she was older now and understood that marriages did break up. But the sight of Tim striding towards them gave her a sense not only of shock, but also of anger. He seemed so very sure of himself.

He came straight up to her. 'You're Janet, aren't you? June couldn't meet the plane. She's frantically busy at the beauty parlour. But she sent me in her stead. How are you, Janet? It's quite a time since we met.' His brown eyes twinkled. There was humour in them as though he were secretly enjoying the situation.

Janet turned and introduced him to Mark Dexter as her sister's husband. As she said it she saw the twinkle in his eyes become malicious. He seemed to regard the situation as a tremendous joke.

'My dear little sister-in-law,' he said. 'What joy it is to welcome you.'

She disliked his expression and the way he said it. Her father had given him hospitality and he had betrayed that hospitality by eloping with his wife. Her father had hated him more than any man in this world. All at once she felt completely in sympathy with her father.

'Are you staying with us? We could manage to put you up for a day or so; or have you arranged to stay somewhere else?'

So she had been right in her feeling they didn't want her in their apartment. A day or two, Tim suggested — a day or two with her mother after eleven years!

Mark interposed. 'I've already arranged for Janet to stay at the Beekman Towers Hotel. It's handy to the office. I'm afraid I'm going to keep her very busy.'

'June and I are busy people, too,' Tim said. 'I'm glad Janet will be kept occupied. I must dash off now; I have an appointment. Will you dine with us tonight, Janet? June is very anxious to see you again. You know the address, of course. We'll be expecting you around half past six.' He said good-bye to both of them and left.

She watched him pushing his way through the crowd. He walked with a slightly swaggering motion.

'So that's your sister's husband,'

Mark remarked. He didn't comment any further.

'What does Mr. Warren do for a living?' Mark asked later, when Janet and he were in a taxi cab heading towards New York.

Janet flushed. 'I don't really know. My sister and I have corresponded infrequently.'

'I think I've seen him more than once out on the racecourse,' Mark said. 'He's a striking-looking man. You told me your sister was much older than you are.'

'A good many years.'

'But Mr. Warren doesn't look much older than thirty,' he commented. 'I gather you're dining with them tonight, so you'll be taken care of. My parents are coming down from Ridgefield, Connecticut, to welcome me. It'll be a sort of family reunion. I would have asked you to come along, Janet, but of course you're anxious to re-meet your sister.'

'Yes,' she said. But all at once she was

dreading it. Tim had come down to the plane to meet her, but he had been off-hand. She felt she wasn't especially welcome — at least, not with him. His suggestion that she stay a day or two in their apartment had been, on the face of it, almost an affront. It was as though he wished her to understand from the beginning there were no close family ties between them.

Mark drove her straight to the Beekman Towers Hotel in Beekman Place on the East River near the United Nations Building. Her room was high up. It was most attractively furnished as a bed-sitting-room. There was a bathroom and small kitchenette. The windows gave her a glorious view out over the city, the crowded city of New York with its skyscrapers and its teeming population.

Mark took her into the cocktail lounge on the top floor where you could get an even better view over the city, over the East River, right on to Brooklyn.

'My apartment is on Park Avenue,' he said. 'Not so far from here. I'll dump my baggage and then call in at the office. I'd like to invite you out to lunch.'

'I quite understand,' she said quickly.

'Do you think you could find your way to the office this afternoon?' he suggested. 'I won't give you any work today, but I should like to introduce you to my office staff. You can lunch in the dining-room here. Or there is an excellent cafeteria.'

'I've always wanted to try an American cafeteria,' she said. 'I'll lunch there.'

He looked at her and his dark grey eyes expressed concern. 'You look tired out, Janet. Why not take a short shut-eye and come to the office around three o'clock?'

She smiled at him. 'It sounds a good idea,' she said. 'And thanks so much for everything, Mark.'

'Bless you, Janet. I only hope you're going to be happy here.'

She didn't draw away from him. His kiss was very sweet. Then he was gone and she was alone in this great vast city. She tried to tell herself that she wasn't hurt that her mother hadn't made the effort to come and meet her no matter how many business appointments she had. Tim Warren was a very poor substitute. She had hated him as a child; she didn't like him now. He was too suave; his manners were too perfect. He never looked you directly in the eye when he spoke to you.

She was glad she was staying at the Beekman Towers Hotel. She wouldn't have liked to live in the penthouse with her mother and Tim Warren.

She lunched at the Beekman Towers cafeteria and bought New York papers to browse over as she ate. They were immense in size compared with the Sydney papers. She glanced briefly through the political news and then became immersed in an article about various daring jewel thefts which had happened recently in New York. Apparently a number of prominent socialites had been robbed of all their jewellery. But as yet the police could make no statement. The robberies had been very cleverly arranged. They had obviously been done by someone who knew their way about the victims' houses. The thieves knew just where the safes were hidden or whether the jewellery was kept in locked caskets in the victims' bedrooms. Some of these robberies had been carried out very daringly while the victims and their guests were dining and the servants were below helping with the meal.

Well, thank heaven I haven't anything anyone would want to steal, she thought, and smiled. The only jewellery she possessed was a string of cultured pearls her father had given her on her eighteenth birthday.

She showered and changed after lunch and then got ready to go to the East-West Publishing Company. It was situated in a modern building on East

Fifty-Third Street, just off Park Avenue. She walked there, enjoying the busy bustle of the streets, admiring the skyscrapers, looking into various shops. She so much wished she had more money to spend here. This was a paradise for women's shopping.

A receptionist at the outer desk, whose name she later learnt was Miss Helen Clune, who operated the switch-board as well, told her that Mr. Dexter was back from lunch and was expecting her. She would take her to his office.

Helen Clune opened the door and said, 'Miss Freeman is here, Mr. Dexter.'

'Well, come in,' Mark said. He rose from behind his desk and extended his hand cordially.

She looked round and almost gasped. Compared with Alvin Harvey's office at the Hamilton Publishing Company, Mark's office was truly magnificent. It was high up in the building and the large windows gave a magnificent view of the city itself and down to the East

River. The furniture was very modern, the desk was large and of polished mahogany. All the walls were lined with bookselves filled with books in their gay paper jackets. She looked round and asked, 'Have you published all these books, Mark?'

'Most of them,' he said. 'Ours is a pretty thriving business, Janet. We have some of the best authors in the States, and some of the most prolific. I'm pretty rushed with appointments this afternoon, but I'll take time off to introduce you to your fellow-members of the staff. We'll first call on Mr. Sam Gleeson; he's my editor-in-chief. I swear he knows the book trade better than any man in New York. His office is right next to this. Come along.'

Mr. Sam Gleeson, a middle-aged man of medium build, with a shock of white hair, was immersed in reading a manuscript, but he stood up as they entered and shook hands cordially with Janet, welcoming her into the firm.

'You'll be working a great deal with

Mr. Gleeson on those Australian manuscripts,' Mark told Janet. 'Now come along and I'll introduce you to Mr. Fred Holstrom, our chief salesman. He's a wizard of a salesman. I swear that there isn't a better one in the whole of the United States.'

Mr. Holstrom was also middle-aged, small and neat and dapper. But one was conscious that he had a powerful driving force, and his smile was charming.

Mark also introduced her to Mr. Peter Winters, the assistant editor, a youngish brown-haired man with pale blue eyes behind large tortoiseshell-framed glasses.

The two girls on the staff were Miss Helen Clune, whom she had already met, who combined the job of receptionist, part-time typist, and operator of the switchboard; and a pretty blonde girl, Miss Julie Green, the secretary Mr. Gleeson and Mark shared between them. Apparently Mr. Holstrom's secretary was on holiday.

'We haven't a very large staff, but I must say it's an efficient one,' Mark told her. 'There's an unused office you can use when you're working here, Janet.'

He showed her into a small attractive room, which also had a lovely view.

'I want you first to go over those manuscripts I brought from Sydney. Make your comments to Mr. Gleeson. Personally I've only looked through them casually. I hadn't much time in Sydney, as you know. But some of them show considerable promise. Not this afternoon,' he added, and laughed. 'I want you to see something of New York. Walk up to Fifth Avenue, stroll along and look at the shops. There is so much to see in New York; stroll through Saks — that's worth seeing. Walk down Forty-second Street with its millions of small shops, take tea at the Algonquin Hotel. That's where all the artistic theatrical and literary lights gather. I only wish I could join you. But I've a pile of work to do. Maybe tomorrow night we could go out and see the town.'

'Are you sure you don't want me to start work today?'

'You'll have a whale of a time discovering New York. Don't miss Bernard Goodmans. They have the classiest clothes. Take a look at the Plaza Hotel and visit Central Park, if you have the time. Tomorrow morning I'll expect you on the job at nine o'clock.'

She wanted very much to see New York, but she was sorry to leave the office. It had a friendly atmosphere and she liked all the people she had met.

She deliberately walked up Fifty-fifth Street and found herself staring at a most impressive shop-front. The window was beautifully and artisically decorated. On the front of the shop were the letters: 'MADAME JUNE BEAUTY SALON.' She stood outside hesitant. She longed to go in and yet she was afraid. Beside, it might be awkward re-meeting her mother amidst a host of strangers. She glanced quickly inside the shop, but saw no one who even faintly resembled her mother as she remembered her. A middle-aged woman with blonde hair that wasn't natural sat behind the reception desk. There were long rows of cubicles and a large glass showcase.

The blonde woman asked, with an over-bright smile, if she could help her. But Janet shook her head. She had a sudden sense of panic. 'No, thank you. I was just looking round,' she stammered and fled back out into the street.

But it was certainly a very high-class beauty parlour. No wonder the socialites patronised it.

When she finally arrived back at the Beekman Towers Hotel she was quite exhausted, thrilled and awed by all she had seen. This was a city of immense buildings, rush and bustle. The life in Sydney seemed very leisurely compared to it. She was astounded by the clothes she had seen — racks and racks of clothes in every possible fitting. Whether you were oversized or slim, you could get exactly what you wanted. In comparison the Sydney shops seemed impoverished. Directly she received her first salary she was determined to buy herself some clothes. She had been particularly attracted by a dinner dress of black tulle and sequins at Saks. It wasn't unreasonably priced, either. Maybe she would take some of the money she had been allowed to bring with her and buy it before she went out with Mark to dinner tomorrow night.

She showered again and changed into a dinner dress she had bought in Sydney. It was a dull green colour and brought out all the copper shades in her pretty head of hair. She dressed very carefully She wanted to look her best to meet her mother. She found her hand was trembling as she applied her make-up. She had never felt so nervous in her whole life before.

She took a taxi to the address in Washington Square. It was a very modern block of flats and had replaced some of the old houses in the Square. The park was full at this twilight hour with couples wandering about and sitting on benches and children playing. It was a small but most attractive square, part of the famous Greenwich Village, where so many artists and writers lived.

Her hand was still shaking as she paid off the taxi cab. She inquired at the reception desk and was told to take the elevator right up to the penthouse. As she made the ascent, she glanced at herself nervously more than once in the mirror. Her face was faintly flushed, but apart from that her appearance was satisfactory; a very pretty young girl, with her small, nicely shaped face, a dimple in her chin, with her bright hazel eyes and longish auburn hair, gazed back at her out of the mirror.

She crossed the small roof-garden with boxes of flowers before she reached the front door of the penthouse. She pressed the bell. It gave a musical chime. Tim Warren opened the door to her. He looked at her and said, 'Well, well, Janet. You certainly look a little more rested than you did when you came off the plane. Come along inside. Your sister June is waiting to meet you.' There was a trace of sardonic humour in his voice and his brown eyes with the amber flecks in them glittered maliciously.

More than ever she found herself disliking him.

There was a woman standing in the room. Janet didn't know who she was. She was short and very slight, extremely smartly dressed. Her hair was jet-black, curled attractively; and the skin of her face was pulled rather tight; her cheeks were rouged. She had heavy mascara on her lashes.

'Janet, my dear sister,' she said. 'You are very welcome.' She went forward and pecked her on the cheek.

Janet was flabbergasted. Her mother was a completely different woman from the one she remembered. She had taken off at least a stone. There was no longer any suggestion of grey in her hair, nor wrinkles under her eyes. Janet had the strangest feeling that this woman was a stranger. She couldn't be her mother. She looked thirty-two, no more. She looked almost the same age as Tim. But for all her make-up, she didn't look well.

'You didn't recognise me.' She sounded pleased. 'I don't look too old to be your sister, do I?'

'You don't look old at all,' Janet said. 'You look quite different somehow.'

'Dear child.' She patted Janet on the hand. 'I couldn't be the famous Madame June if I didn't know how to look after my own self. You're very welcome here. I'm very glad to see you.' But they might have been strangers. Stranger than strangers, Janet thought.

But the very fact that her mother looked different made it easier for her to fall into the younger sister deception. She didn't feel she was her mother any longer; she might have been a sister she had seen briefly in her youth.

Tim might have left them alone for a few minutes, but apparently he had no intention of doing so. He stood in the background watching the scene, the same sardonic humour in his eyes.

'I would have asked you to stay here,' June said, 'but we have very little room and, typical of New York these days, very little help. Tim does the cooking and we have a coloured maid to clean up in the mornings. We have invited a few friends in tonight to meet you. They'll be with us after dinner. Some of the girls who work in the beauty salon; we're all close friends there. And some men friends of Tim's. Tim told me you were staying at the Beekman Towers Hotel. Are you quite happy there?'

She nodded. 'Very happy. It's a lovely hotel and close enough so that I can walk to the office.'

'That's simply splendid,' June said. Her voice was brittle, almost staccato, and Janet suddenly realised that her mother was as nervous about this meeting as she had been — as she still was. Were they to keep up the farce of sister relationship between themselves? But how would that be possible? She didn't think her mother looked at all well, either.

She wished Tim would go and leave her mother and herself alone together so they could talk. But he was pouring cocktails from a corner bar in the luxuriously furnished sitting-room. Janet noticed he was watching them both closely. The situation appeared to amuse him hugely.

Janet found herself hating him more than ever. He had wrecked her father's life; he had taken her mother from her when she was a child and needed her most. But all he seemed to feel was a sardonic amusement at the situation.

She drank the cocktail he handed her. She was so shaken she felt she needed it. She even accepted another, though she rarely drank more than one. But the drink soothed her nerves, gave her courage — courage enough to say to her mother before dinner, 'I'd like to tidy up. Can I go to your room?'

'I'll show you the way,' June said.

Tim spoke sharply. 'There's no need for you to go, June. The bedroom is on the right just down the corridor. It has a connecting bathroom.'

Apparently he was determined not to leave her alone with her mother. Did he think she'd make a scene, burst into tears? But at the moment she almost felt as though she had no emotions.

The dining-room adjoined the living-room. It had a long oak table with green-velvet-upholstered chairs. The rugs on a parquet floor were Persian. Tim had cooked a delicious lobster casserole. There was cold chicken, ham, and salad to follow.

During the meal they asked her questions about her trip. She remembered that Julian had told her that he knew Tim. She mentioned his name as having met him in Australia and then later on the plane from Nadi to New York.

'Julian Gaden? I shouldn't say he was

a bosom friend of mine, but we're quite friendly. He seems to have the knack of suddenly appearing — sometimes when he isn't wanted,' Tim added.

'Yes, he does turn up at the oddest times,' Janet agreed.

'And it isn't always easy to shake him off,' Tim went on. 'Several times I've tried to get rid of him quietly and easily, but he has the knack of hanging on. I'd very much like to know what he does for a living.'

Janet felt the same about Tim. What did he do? Did he live on her mother's earnings at the beauty salon? Was cooking his sole contribution to the upkeep of this expensive penthouse?

She mentioned she had met Coleen Hausman in Honolulu and that she was a friend of her employer, Mark Dexter.

'Did she come back in the plane with you?' Tim asked rather sharply. 'I didn't see her at the airport.'

'No. She's staying on a few extra days in Honolulu,' Janet said.

'She comes to the beauty salon at

times,' June said. 'And at other times various of our assistants go and dress her hair and give her a beauty treatment in the flat. I've been there myself several times. They have to pay twice as much for my services,' June went on with a touch of pride. 'But most of my clients think it worth it. Coleen Hausman stinks of money.'

'Did her husband leave her much? Janet asked.

Tim laughed. 'He hadn't much to leave her. Henry Hausman had nothing but a talent for writing, and good looks. He wasn't awfully clever, but he was a decent sort. But he could never keep pace with Coleen. She tires of men and casts them aside as if they were old shoes.' He leant further across the table. 'By the way, was she wearing the famous Cameron Emeralds in Honolulu?'

'I didn't see her wearing any emeralds. She did wear a diamond necklet and diamonds in her ears. Are the Cameron Emeralds famous?'

'They're worth a fortune,' Tim said. 'They were left her by her mother, Clarice Cameron.'

'She's very careless with her jewellery,' June commented. 'When I've been there to give her a hair-do and a facial, jewellery is always lying around in heaps on the dressing-table. But then why should she care — it's probably heavily insured. Besides, one day she will inherit her father's millions.'

'How did she strike you as a person?' Tim sounded interested.

'I didn't like her very much,' Janet conceded. 'She's spoilt and wilful.'

Tim looked amused. 'And she's after your employer, Mark Dexter, isn't she? I happened to see an item in a gossip column. Besides, it's more or less current knowledge in Café Society that at some date in the near future Coleen means to become Mrs. Mark Dexter.'

Janet's heart missed a beat. She felt sick and wretched. She had an uncomfortable feeling that Tim Warren knew just how she felt and was enjoying the situation.

When Tim was in the kitchen preparing coffee, her mother leant across the table and said to her in a low voice, 'You must see that it's impossible I should claim to be anything but your sister, Janet? Tim's so young. It would hurt his pride if it were known he had a wife so much older than himself.'

'Then the sister idea was Tim's?' Janet asked.

Her mother nodded. 'He has a youth complex. He convinced himself I'm as young as I appear. He couldn't bear to have a stepdaughter. He said it would make him feel like a grandfather in a bath-chair.'

'I don't mind,' Janet said. 'Though I admit I was hurt and bewildered at first.'

'I hurt you very badly, didn't I, Janet?' June said sadly. 'As a child you must have suffered considerably. I was selfish, I suppose, but I was so madly in love with Tim. He was all that mattered. He is all that matters to me now.'

'I shall try and understand,' Janet said in a low voice. 'But you're not at all as I remember you.'

'I had grey hairs at thirty,' June Warren said. 'It was Tim who first insisted I dye my hair. When I went to the beauty parlour to have it done and have my face attended to, I became interested in the work. I took a year's training and then Tim suddenly made a large sum of money on the stock exchange and we opened up the Madame June Beauty Salon. It prospered from the start. I don't really know why, but today it's an established success.'

'Does Tim help you in the salon?' Janet asked.

June shook her head and smiled. 'Oh, no. He has his own affairs to attend to. The man who works with me is Monsieur Charles, besides the other girls, Cicely, Renée and Carmen. You must come and have a beauty treatment with me, Janet. I could smarten up your hair, do something for your skin — not that you need much in the way of beauty treatments. You're young and an extremely pretty child. I've thought about you quite a lot,' June added, dropping her voice almost to a whisper.

'I've thought about you, too,' Janet said. 'Ever since Daddy died. I've always wanted to meet you again.'

'It was very sad, your father's death. I hope he had some happy years before he died.'

Janet shook her head. 'Daddy was never happy after you left him' — she was about to say 'Mother,' but changed it quickly to 'June.'

Tim was back in the room with the coffee. 'The others will be arriving at any moment now. The girls are coming from the beauty parlour with Monsieur Charles and Madame Claire. I've invited some pals of my own — Horace Greenslip, Reggie Fallow and Ben Swartz.'

'I don't like Ben Swartz,' June said.

Her voice was sharp, staccato.

Tim smiled that easy, loose smile of his. 'Oh, Ben's all right, June. He's a good friend to me — a very clever fellow.'

'Sometimes I wonder if he isn't too clever,' June remarked.

'You must let me be the judge of my own friends.' He sounded faintly angry.

'Of course, my dearest, of course,' June said quickly. There was a note in her voice Janet didn't like to hear — a note approaching fear.

June had said that she loved Tim. But was she also afraid of him? Was that why she had never invited Janet over to stay with her? Why her reply to Janet's cable had been so cool?

But already the guests were starting to arrive, coming in in laughing groups. The girls from the beauty shop were all slick and pretty, their hair styles perfect, their make-up attractive.

She met Madame Claire, the blonde woman she had seen at the reception desk at the beauty salon. Madame

Claire looked at her curiously, as though she half recognised her but couldn't remember where they had met.

Monsieur Charles was effeminate and dapper. He wore a light grey lounge suit, a bright green pullover and black suede shoes. He had a boy friend with him, whom he called Maurice. He didn't seem much interested in the girls, but perhaps he saw too much of them in the beauty salon.

Other guests arrived. Janet's head was spinning trying to remember their names. They all seemed to know each other. Janet felt rather out of things. She wished she had been able to spend the evening alone with her mother, even if Tim insisted upon being present. He seemed jealous of allowing them any time alone together.

It was a warm night and half the party had drifted out into the penthouse garden with its bright boxes of flowers and magnificent views. Tim was playing host behind the bar and June was helping him. Janet felt she would be happier doing something. She might at least hand round the canapés.

She was just going into the kitchen to fetch a fresh tray of canapés when suddenly she heard a voice she knew so well: ‘Hello, Tim! Hello, June!’ It was Julian Gaden. ‘I’m afraid I’ve gate-crashed this party. I hope you’re not going to throw me out on my ear.’

# 11

'I didn't send you an Invitation,' Tim said gruffly. 'But since you're here, you may as well stay. I gather you met my sister-in-law in Sydney.'

'I sure did,' Julian said. 'We also travelled on the plane from Nadi and made a brief stop-over in Honolulu owing to engine trouble. I wanted to see how the kid was getting on in the big city.' He chuckled and added, 'I'm glad you're not going to throw me out, Tim.'

Tim shrugged. He managed a smile. 'It wouldn't be much use, would it, Julian? You'd only reappear in five minutes or so, wearing a wig, a false moustache and using an assumed name. I doubt if half the parties you go to, you bother to get yourself invited.'

It was almost rude the way he said it, but Julian merely grinned. 'I go where I want to go. I admit I don't always bother asking for an invitation. Where is Janet?'

'She's gone into the kitchen to fetch some canapés,' Tim said. His voice was over-casual. He was obviously annoyed.

'I'll rout her out,' Julian said. 'She ought to be out on the patio, looking out over the brilliantly sparkling lights of New York.'

Janet had overheard part of this conversation before she had disappeared into the kitchen. Her cheeks were flushed with embarrassment, but she felt happier. Everyone here was so very strange — even her own mother. She felt Julian was her friend.

She was standing by the kitchen table when Julian came in.

'Hello, Janet! Pleased to see me?' Suddenly he caught her in his arms. He kissed her on the lips. 'I'm crazy about you, Janet,' he said. 'That's why I gate-crashed this party tonight. I felt you might need support. Tim's friends are rather curious people.'

'How do you mean curious?'

'On the borderline.' He shrugged. 'I warned you against coming here, didn't I? I warn you now; don't get mixed up with any of Tim's friends and associates.'

'But you're a friend of his,' she pointed out.

'I think he'd have liked to chuck me out. But Tim doesn't want to offend anyone — especially anyone who might be too nosey about his business interests.'

'I wish you wouldn't talk like that. You make me' — she hesitated — 'afraid.'

He said in a low tense voice, 'I'm afraid for you, Janet. It would be healthier for you to mix with Café Society with Mark Dexter.'

'And have Coleen Hausman always at my elbow?'

'Well, she's in Honolulu now. I hope you're making some progress with Mark?'

She flushed. 'He's been very busy all

day. I took myself out on a sightseeing excursion.'

'I wish I'd known. I'd like to have been along. Why didn't you phone me like you phoned me that afternoon in Honolulu? It sure gave me a thrill.'

'I don't know where to get in touch with you.'

'I've got a small apartment in the East Sixties. It's not much of a place, but it's enough for a bachelor like me. I shouldn't wish you luck with Mark; I want you so badly for myself; but I do wish you luck. May I kiss you again, Janet?'

She let him kiss her. She liked him so much as a friend. There were moments when he held her in his arms when she even liked him better than as a friend. But there was always Mark; she loved Mark.

When they reappeared in the lounge more guests had just arrived. There was chatter and shrill laughter everywhere. Tim saw that the drinks kept circulating. She supposed she should be grateful to Tim and her mother throwing this party for her, but it was the last thing she had wanted.

She tried to have some further conversation with her mother, but it was next to impossible. Tim, like a dark shadow, always seemed to come between them. Was he afraid that she would give the secret away? Was he really so vain that he couldn't bear the thought that people knew he had a wife so much older than himself?

Julian and she wandered out on to the patio.

'And what do you think of New York?' he asked her.

'It's a fascinating and intoxicating city. I've never seen such tall buildings, so much rush and bustle. People here must live very much on their nerves.'

'They do,' he told her seriously. 'Most of the women drink too much and the majority of the business men have ulcers. Have they introduced you to a character called Ben Swartz?'

'I met him earlier in the evening — a

carroty-haired little man.'

'He's served a prison term,' Julian told her. 'He could crack a safe as well as anyone in New York. But lately he appears to have been going straight.' He added sardonically, 'Tim Warren has a big heart. An erstwhile crook who wants to make the grade back into decent society can always expect a helping hand from him. This, as I said, is a very borderline society.'

She had some sudden sense of fear, not for herself but for her mother. She gathered from Julian's remarks that Tim was involved in some sort of racket. But what racket? And how far did it involve her mother?

'You've never seen Broadway with all the lights on, have you?' Julian said presently. 'Will you let me drive you home? We'll do a detour along Broadway.'

'I'd love to go,' she said. 'I've been meeting so many people here my head is spinning.'

'Let's go soon. I haven't a great deal

of time for the set Tim mingles with.'

She told her mother she was tired and that Julian would drive her home. For a moment a suggestion of tears glittered in her mother's eyes. 'My dear, it has been nice to know you again. Keep in touch. Tim and I are at home most evenings. I'm so exhausted after a day in the beauty salon, I don't go out very much. I haven't felt very well lately. But won't you look in at the salon? I'll have Cicely — one of my best assistants — make you look swell.'

She said on an impulse, 'Perhaps I could come in tomorrow, at the lunch hour? I have an important dinner date.'

She said good-bye to Tim.

'So Julian Gaden is driving you home,' he said. 'He must be pretty keen, since he gate-crashed this party. But then I think I said at dinner he was always turning up at the oddest places, half of the time when he's not wanted. Don't go losing your heart to him, Janet. He's a very odd character.'

Broadway, with its myriad lights and signs, was spectacular at night. They left the taxi at Times Square and walked up Broadway towards Central Park. She found they were holding hands, but she didn't mind. The crowd was so intense she might otherwise have lost him. It was not only the flashing signs overhead; all the shops too were brilliantly lighted. It was as bright as daylight. They looked up at the signs, they peered into shop windows; the whole of Broadway had a gay carnival atmosphere. They were jostled here and there, but good-humouredly jostled. All the bars were wide open with people milling in and out.

Presently they reached Central Park. A line of old-fashioned carriages was drawn beside the Plaza Hotel for those who wished to take a drive through the park in the moonlight.

'Let's climb into a carriage and make a night of it,' Julian said.

She hesitated. 'I'm rather tired.'

'You can lean against my shoulder

and go to sleep. I don't want to lose you tonight, Janet.'

It was lovely driving through the park, the soft lights showing between the trees, the moon full overhead, the sky a basketful of stars.

'You're glad I gate-crashed that party this evening?' he asked her urgently.

She whispered, 'Very glad. But I'm awfully sleepy, Julian. I didn't sleep well on the plane last night.'

'But I told you to lay your head on my shoulder and go to sleep now. I just want to have you close to me.'

He put his arm about her shoulder. But sleep didn't come immediately.

Presently, though, her head slipped sideways and against his shoulder. She felt a sudden sense of peace. All the perplexities she had come up against seemed straightened out. She closed her eyes.

She must have slept for some little time. When she awoke his arm was close about her. She heard him whisper, 'My darling. My dearest Janet.'

Mark had once called her my darling, but only once. Most of the time in Honolulu he had been taken up with Coleen. What would happen when Coleen got back to New York? But she was too sleepy to think about it that night. She felt curiously at peace, as though she belonged in Julian's arms.

It was very late when they got back to the Beekman Towers Hotel. She had awoken somewhat, in the taxi cab which drove them from the park to the East River. He went into the lobby with her and wrote down his phone number. 'I'll be seeing you,' he said. 'But call me any time; any time you're lonesome, Janet; any time you're afraid.'

She opened her hazel eyes wide and asked, 'What have I to be afraid of, Julian?'

'You were afraid tonight. I felt fear and tension in you. You don't like Tim Warren, do you?'

'No, I don't.'

'He's a pretty slick customer. He may be in love with your sister June, but apart from that, I don't think he gives a damn for anybody. He didn't tell you what he did for a living, I suppose?'

She countered, 'What do *you* do for a living, Julian?'

He grinned at her. 'I watch other people. And that sounds phoney, doesn't it? At the moment I'm watching after you. I don't like your association with Tim and your elder sister. Do we have a date tomorrow night?'

'I'm going out with Mark.'

'Making hay while Coleen's in Honolulu?' He grinned again. 'I've warned you not to underestimate that dame.'

'I don't underestimate her, but I don't think Mark's in love with her. That's all in the past.'

'I wouldn't be too sure. Coleen Hausman can be pretty persuasive. But good luck to you. I wish you loved me as you love Mark.'

He was gone and she was alone in the foyer of the vast hotel. She went up to her room and got wearily out of her clothes. She stood for a few minutes by the window in her sheer nylon nightdress, looking over New York city and the East River. She had re-met her mother, but her mother seemed a different person from how she remembered her. She longed for a grey-haired, full-bosomed mother who was kind and understanding. June thought only of Tim; and yet Janet sensed she was afraid of Tim. She yawned and climbed into bed.

But she didn't sleep at once. How long had she slept with her head resting on Julian's shoulder? She had been through so much nervous tension that night, she had felt exhausted. His presence had been a great comfort to her.

'I don't care what anyone says about him, I like him.' She said the words aloud. Then she smiled and snuggled up between the sheets. Julian was her friend. The thought gave her courage.

# 12

She presented herself for work at nine the following morning. Mark greeted her with his usual attractive smile and asked if she would like to start reading through the Australian manuscripts.

She smiled back at him. 'Of course. That's what I'm here for, isn't it?'

'I only took a cursory glance through them in Sydney,' he said, 'but some of them seemed to have worthwhile stuff in them. Rather sordid — and that's strange, for Australia is a beautiful country. Most of the writers seem to have a faintly left-wing tinge. You must be careful of that. We don't like leftist writers over here. But with the authors' permission we can re-edit some of them. If you find a particularly good manuscript, pass it over to Sam Gleeson.'

The first book she started on was an

adventure story laid in New Guinea and the Pacific Islands. It had strength, and obviously the author knew well the countries he was writing about. She was left alone in her office; there was no mid-morning tea break such as they had in Australia. Before she knew it, it was lunch time and she had an appointment in the beauty salon. She wondered what they would do to her appearance and how Mark would like it. It would be an adventure, anyhow.

June welcomed her and said, 'My dear, I'm so glad you were able to make it. Monsieur Charles is going to take you for the haircut and set, then Renée Florell will give you a beauty treatment.' June touched her hand. It was a lingering, rather pathetic gesture. 'You won't know yourself once we've finished with you, my dear.'

She had met Monsieur Charles last night. She hadn't liked him particularly. She had considered him effeminate. But he obviously was past-master of his trade. Usually she wore her hair long, but he cut it considerably shorter, stylised it and then one of the girls shampooed her and he came back to do the set.

While she was still in rollers, Renée Florell, a pretty girl, brown-haired, dark grey eyes, short and ultra-smart looking, came in to give her a facial. She plucked her eye-brows, she massaged her face and put on a mask. She had to lie there in the darkness until the mask was finally removed. Then Renée made her up very skilfully. She had looked a pretty girl before; now she looked both pretty and sophisticated.

When Monsieur Charles had finished her hair she looked a different person.

June came in and smiled at her. 'You look wonderful, my dear.'

Janet laughed. 'I'll have to get used to my appearance over again. I only hope Mark will like the change.'

June looked at her with interest. 'He's your boss? The man who brought you over to the States. You must introduce him to us, Janet.'

'I'd like to,' Janet said. But she wasn't sure she wanted Mark to meet Tim Warren again.

'Is he attractive?' June asked.

Janet flushed. 'Very attractive.'

June looked at her with added interest. 'I think you're a little keen on him, aren't you, my dear? Tim and I were afraid that Julian Gaden was the man. He really had a nerve gate-crashing the party last night and carrying you off. Tim was furious. Tim takes violent likes and dislikes to people. I think it would be better if you didn't bring him to the house again. Your employer, Mr. Dexter, is quite a different matter. I've heard Mrs. Hausman speak of him. Rumours have been going round that ultimately they'll make a marriage.'

'I know,' Janet said. 'I read an item in a gossip column. But I don't really think that Mark wants to marry her.'

June sighed. 'I hope for your sake he doesn't, Janet. But she is very beautiful and very rich.'

'But should that mean so much to a man like Mark?' Janet argued. 'He has his job and apparently plenty of money besides.'

'Has he said anything to you about marriage?'

Janet hesitated. 'No, not exactly. But I know he likes me.'

They were alone in one of the attractively decorated cubicles and her mother embraced her briefly and rather timidly. 'Good luck, my dear. I hope you have a splendid time tonight.'

She was late in returning to the office and full of apologies. Mark was the first to notice her altered appearance.

'What on earth have you been doing to yourself, Janet?' He sounded rather angry.

'I had a hair-do and a beauty treatment in the lunch hour,' she told him. She asked a little wistfully, 'Don't you like it? I wanted to look specially good tonight when I went out with you.'

His smile forgave her. 'I suppose I

was a little stunned by your changed appearance. You've always looked so natural, so fresh. Sophisticated women are two-a-penny in New York. I think I preferred you as you were.'

'I'm sorry, Mark.' She could have wept.

'Don't forget I'm calling for you at the Beekman Towers Hotel at seven o'clock.'

'As if I should forget.' She gave him a small smile.

'Now get back to your manuscript,' he said. 'How's it going?'

'I think it's good. It's quick and fast-moving, and the author evidently knows his stuff.'

'I thought so too, from the little I've read of it. Now back to work.'

She had wanted to buy the dinner dress, but she hadn't had time. She would have to wear one of the dresses she had brought with her from Australia.

It was a pretty dress, black faille with a scalloped hem. It seemed to suit the hair-do and the way Renée Florell had made up her face.

* * *

'I'd like to show you my flat,' Mark said, when he met her. 'We'll have a cocktail there before going on. You look very pretty and sophisticated tonight, Janet, and I'm not minding that new hair-do half so much. Would you like to dine at the Stork Club? It's fashionable with Café Society and most of the top-notch artistes patronise it.'

She was excited. 'I've heard so much about the Stork Club. Do you think my dress is all right for it, Mark?'

'Of course.' He smiled back at her and took one of her hands. 'You look enchanting.'

They took a taxi up to Mark's apartment on Park Avenue. 'I don't use my car in the city,' he told her. 'The parking problem is too troublesome. But when I drive you out into the country to Ridgefield, Connecticut, to meet my parents I'll drive you in the Cadillac.'

She was thrilled at the thought that he should want her to meet his parents. It showed he didn't regard her merely as a member of the firm . . . or a pretty girl to be kissed on a moonlight night in the tropics.

'It's a typically bachelor flat,' Mark said as he showed her in at the door. 'But I have some rather nice old Colonial antiques I've picked up on my drives through Connecticut. On the road up to Ridgefield every second house sells antiques. You have to be pretty sharp to know which are genuine and which are not.'

It was a lovely apartment with big windows looking down over Park Avenue. There was parquet flooring with Persian rugs. They went with the Colonial antiques. The draperies were a deep scarlet. There were drinks on thc sideboard. He asked her what she'd have, but when she said a sherry, he protested: 'Not a sherry tonight, Janet darling. A dry martini is the right set-off for an evening like this.'

Once again he had called her darling and her heart lifted and beat faster.

They clicked their glasses together and drank. She refused a second drink, but he had another. Then he put his glass down on the sideboard. His hands were slightly unsteady.

'Darling, I'm going to kiss you. Do you mind? But you wouldn't have come up here if you really minded, would you, Janet?'

Colour stained her cheeks. Perhaps she shouldn't have come up to his apartment.

'Darling,' he laughed hoarsely, 'don't be bashful. I only want a kiss. I'm not going to harm you.'

She let him take her in his arms because she wanted to go into them. She felt his kisses hot on her mouth, her cheeks, her throat. His hands slid down her back to draw her closer to him.

Suddenly she was scared. Was Mark used to having his way with women?

She drew away. Her voice was shaking. 'Please, Mark, no more.'

'You really mean that, Janet? You don't want me to make love to you tonight?'

'No,' she said, and she had a sense of despair. Was that all he wanted with her — to make love? Had he no intention of marrying her?

He laughed, and this time he kissed her softly on the cheek. 'I've scared you, haven't I? I'm sorry, darling. I guess despite that sophisticated hair-do, you're still as young and naïve as you ever were. Let's go out, shall we, and have dinner?'

She was grateful to him for understanding. He hadn't tried to force her love. He had called her darling several times, but he had made no suggestion of marriage. Was she truly young and naïve? Too young and naïve for the sophisticated society Mark moved in? Would Coleen have responded more warmly to his embrace?

Damn Coleen! She thought. She

wasn't going to let her spoil this night out together.

The Stork Club was crowded as usual, but the head waiter knew Mark and found them a table. Mark seemed to have a host of friends dining there. They all greeted him and many came across to his table. He introduced them to Janet, telling her who they were when they had left the table. They were mostly members of the famous Café Society. He pointed out several theatrical, film and TV stars. She felt heady and excited. She had never dreamt of herself in such an important gathering.

There was music playing, but they didn't dance.

'We'll do our dancing afterwards at the Copacabana night club,' he said.

Mark excused himself to go over and talk to some old friends. It was then that she saw Tim dining with Ben Swartz and Reggie Fallow. But where was June? Did Tim often leave her alone of an evening?

He caught her eyes, waved and

smiled. She had to admit he was an undeniably handsome-looking man with his muscular shoulders, his waving brown hair, his brown eyes with the amber flecks in them.

He came across to her. 'I didn't expect to see you here, Janet. Who's your cavalier?'

'Mark Dexter.'

'Your publisher? The guy who it's rumoured is going to marry Coleen Hausman?'

She didn't want to discuss that subject. 'Where's June?' she asked him.

'She was tired and went to bed. She hasn't been at all well lately, I'm afraid. I brought my pals along. I like this place. The people who dine here are the tops.'

Mark returned to the table. He invited Tim to join them in a drink. Tim accepted over-eagerly.

He's a snob, she thought. A social climber. And she liked him less than ever. He fawned upon Mark in a rather odious way. Janet was greatly relieved when he left them.

'What does your sister's husband do for a living?' Mark inquired.

She remembered he had asked her that question before, and still she couldn't reply.

'I don't really know. I gather he has business interests in the city.'

'And your sister runs the Madame June Beauty Salon, where they took away my dear unsophisticated little Janet and made her look something quite different. I still don't know whether I like you in your new guise. You look like Coleen Hausman or a hundred other women in Café Society.'

'But Coleen is really lovely.'

He gave a short laugh. 'She certainly works hard enough at it. She must be twenty-six or seven, and no woman — especially a woman like Coleen — wants to look her age. But it's different with you, Janet — you have youth. You have what all the other women crave.'

She smiled across at him. 'It's nice to

hear you say things like that, Mark. It makes me feel as close to you as I did in Sydney.'

'You didn't feel the same in Honolulu?'

'How could I? Coleen Hausman seemed to own you.'

He chuckled. 'Maybe she thinks she does. We've been friends so long; sweethearts once. There have been times, even fairly recently, when I have thought it wouldn't be such a bad marriage. But if I married Coleen, I would lose you, Janet.' He took both her hands under the table and squeezed them tightly.

She saw Tim had seen the gesture. He winked across at her in a sardonic way. She wished she hadn't run into him here. His presence seemed to spoil things. She was pleased when Mark suggested they go on to the Copacabana. There would be dancing, and she loved to dance with Mark. She felt she was floating in his arms, the soft music twining itself around her feet.

'Next week-end, if you're free, we'll drive out into the country to Ridgefield,' Mark said. 'I want to show my parents my new little assistant from Down Under.'

It was late when they left the Copacabana.

'Will you kiss me to forgive me for taking you too much for granted?' he whispered. 'I shouldn't have done it, Janet, not with you. Most girls don't object to a little petting.'

'I forgive you, Mark. You've given me a wonderful evening.' She kissed him readily on the lips.

'Bless you, my darling. I have a strange feeling I might easily fall in love with you.'

* * *

The next day she dropped in at the lunch hour at the Madame June Beauty Salon. She felt that with Tim always around the apartment this was the only opportunity she could get to see her mother again. She craved some sign of her affection. Once or twice it had been given to her, but timidly; never when Tim Warren was about. She suspected he had a very jealous nature; he wanted all June's attention for himself. He didn't want to share it with her, June's daughter. She sensed that while he tried to make himself pleasant, he secretly resented her.

She had thought she could be indifferent to her mother; she might even dislike her, after all she had made her and her father suffer through her childhood. But she couldn't dislike her. She felt a strong sense of warmth when she was with her. She longed for her mother to embrace her, admit she was her daughter. She would have liked to tell her mother all about her love for Mark. Mark had said last night he thought he might easily fall in love with her. But was that just flattery at the end of an amusing evening?

But at the beauty salon Miss Mary Claire, the receptionist, told her that

Madame June was indisposed that day. She was in bed in the apartment.

Janet promised herself she would go down to the Washington Square penthouse as soon as she left work. Her mother might look young, with those little scars behind her ears which showed she had had her face lifted several times, but she was no longer very young. And Tim and she led a very strenuous life.

Mark left the office early. He said he had to attend a round of cocktail parties. 'Most of them are publishing houses,' he told her. 'This is the season for authors bringing out new books. You have to put in an appearance; they might think you were jealous that you didn't get the manuscript yourself.' He smiled at her. 'You will be all right tonight Janet? You won't be lonely?'

She had finished the manuscript on the South Pacific. She would make notes on it tomorrow and then hand them and the manuscript over to Sam Gleeson.

She took the bus down Fifth Avenue to Washington Square and walked across to the apartment building where Tim and June had the penthouse. A coloured maid, who seemed on the point of leaving, let her in. 'Mrs. is in the bedroom,' she said. 'She sure is sick.'

Janet hurried into the bedroom. 'June,' she cried. 'Oh June, how are you? I went into the beauty parlour at lunch-time and they told me that you were home in bed.'

Her mother's face was grey. She almost looked her age. She had been crying. She hastily brushed the tears aside.

Janet impulsively threw her arms about her. 'Darling,' she said. 'You don't look well.'

'I'll be all right soon,' June said. 'I get these turns now and again. I don't know what causes them.'

'Haven't you seen a doctor?' Janet asked.

She shook her head. 'I'd hate Tim to

think that I was a sick woman. He's so full of health and high spirits himself. I have to keep pace with him; I must.' She set her teeth, her voice rasped slightly.

'Why must you, darling? Surely Tim knows you are several years older than he is. He must make allowances.'

'But he won't,' June said. 'He hates invalids of any sort. He might even leave me, Janet. I couldn't bear that. I couldn't bear it.' She shuddered.

'Do you love him so much?' Janet asked gently.

'I love him more than anything in this world. I'd kill myself if he ever left me.'

Janet was shocked. Her mother's voice was half hysterical. Presently she went on: 'I gave up everything for him. You, Janet, and a kind, protective husband. But Tim is something quite different. I knew from the first moment I met him, I couldn't live without him.' She clutched at Janet's arm. 'Don't ever love a man as much as that. It isn't good; it isn't healthy. It makes a wreck of you trying to keep up with him all the time. Tim's been out all day. He doesn't like me when I'm sick.'

'May I stay with you tonight, June?' Janet asked humbly. 'I'll make supper for both of us, if you'll let me.'

There was sudden fear in June's eyes, and her voice was shaken as she said, 'Tim mightn't like it.'

'I can take care of Master Tim,' Janet said angrily. 'I'm not going to leave you alone in your present condition. I still think you should see a doctor.'

'No, please no, my dearest girl,' June begged. 'And I don't think you should stay on here this evening. If Tim comes home he might think . . . '

'Let him think what he wishes.' Janet's voice was still tart and angry. 'I'm not going to leave you here alone in the apartment, when you're so sick, without any supper.'

'Tim may not be back until much later tonight,' June said. 'He has work to do. Get some supper for yourself, child, and get me a hot lemon drink.

Tim may not be back until all hours. You'll be gone by then.'

Janet was fighting mad as she got them some supper. Tim might resent her, but he couldn't cut her entirely off from her mother. She thought of Tim's rather pallid good looks, his waving brown hair, his lighter brown eyes. He was like a child who had never grown up, making constant demands on June. She was both his mother and his wife.

There was the noise of the front door opening. Tim's voice called from the lounge: 'It all went off like clockwork, darling. Couldn't have been easier. A child could have done it.'

Her mother's voice called, and now there was definite fear in it, 'Tim, Janet is here.'

Tim came in smiling his self-sufficient smile. 'Oh hello, Janet. Come to keep your mother company? I was otherwise engaged — a bet upon the trotters.' But he made the explanation almost too casually. His brown eyes were hard as they looked at Janet. 'I'll take care of June now. You're free to go out and enjoy yourself. Which man will you choose for tonight — Mark Dexter or that gate-crasher Julian Gaden?'

'I'm not going anywhere tonight,' Janet said. 'I'm going home to bed. I was late last night and there's a lot of work I have to do at the office.'

'Your boss Mark Dexter seems pretty keen on you,' Tim said. 'Are you going to marry him, Janet?'

She flushed furiously. 'As yet there's been no suggestion of marriage.'

'He'll be a wily bird to catch,' Tim warned her. 'Twenty-eight, a publishing house, and private money. You may succeed. I wish you luck. He's a better bet than Julian Gaden.'

She found herself resenting his remark and the way he said it.

'I like Julian,' she said coldly.

'But he's a no-good oaf, picking up a job here and there. I hear he chaperoned a rock-'n'-roll star out to Sydney. Jobs like that — a thrower-out.'

Janet got to her feet. It was all too

apparent now that Tim very much resented her association with her mother. 'I'll go home now, but I do think June should see a doctor.'

He gave a great guffaw of laughter. 'See a doctor? Why, she's as sound as a bell. Been drinking too much at these recent parties, that's the trouble.' He added ingratiatingly, 'I'm sure glad you called tonight, Janet. I'll look after June now.'

He seemed eager for her to go. What had he begun to tell her mother as his voice drifted across the sitting-room? Something to the effect it had all been easy, a child could have done it. Done what? What had he been talking about?

She left the penthouse almost hurriedly, as though she was fleeing from some unpleasant knowledge. Tim didn't want her presence. Was he afraid of her influence upon her mother? But Janet felt she had no influence; her mother was wholly and entirely wrapped up in Tim.

She saw Julian Gaden's number lying on her dressing-table. She hesitated, and then on an impulse she called him.

His voice responded quickly. 'Who is that?'

'Janet,' she said. 'I'm just signing off for tonight but I just wanted to say good night to you.'

'Mighty sweet of you. I suppose it's too late to call round?'

'Much too late. I'm going straight to bed. Good night, Julian.'

'Good night, Janet, my darling. Bless you.'

She had Mark's number, but it didn't occur to her to telephone him. She would have felt embarrassed. He might think she was pushing the pace too much, that she had read more into those words he had said last night than he had meant. She would have to wait. But it was so hard waiting; Coleen Hausman might be back at any moment.

* * *

She woke late, dressed quickly, had a cup of coffee standing by the cafeteria bar, rushed up to the office. Mark was already at his desk, reading the morning papers.

'Have you seen the papers?' he asked her urgently.

She shook her head. 'I didn't have time to read them.'

'Coleen's apartment was ransacked last night. It must have been after the daily maid left. The maid, when she returned in the morning, called the police. They contacted Colonel John Cameron immediately. The wall safe had been opened. The famous Cameron Emeralds, left to Coleen by her mother, have been stolen.'

Janet gave a small gasp and sank down into a chair. 'The emeralds have been stolen, Mark?'

He nodded grimly. 'They were well insured, of course, but they had a great sentimental value for Coleen. She told me that was why she hadn't taken them to Honolulu with her. She thought they would be safer locked in the safe in her apartment. It was very cunningly concealed behind a picture-and-flower arrangement.'

'Someone must have known the layout of the apartment,' Janet whispered.

He nodded again. 'And also that Coleen was away. She didn't have a resident help, but two series of housemaids — one in the day and one at night. But she laid off the one at night when she went to Honolulu.'

Janet found herself shaking with an awful sense of fear. But the robbery could have nothing to do with what she had said to Tim; nothing to do with Tim's first words last night when he came into the apartment. Why did she even think such a thing? It was enough to dislike a man, it was dreadful to accuse him even in your thoughts of theft.

She determined to put the idea right out of her mind.

'Does Coleen know yet?'

'Her father telephoned her at the Royal Hawaiian. She said she would fly right back. Not that her presence here can help much. The New York police are doing all that is possible. But I guess she wants to come back at this time.'

She would have liked to say, 'She wouldn't be finding Honolulu so attractive without your presence, Mark. Not even Leslie Henderson could compensate for that.'

'I'm meeting her plane tomorrow. I hoped to take you out to dinner, Janet, but that's it.'

'But you must meet her, Mark?' She asked it as a question.

He flushed slightly. 'She'd consider it very unfriendly if I wasn't there to meet her. After all, she flew out all the way to Honolulu to meet me.'

'I understand, Mark.' But she felt miserable and dispirited as she went back into her lonely office. Could she never escape from Coleen or the hold she had over Mark from their being childhood sweethearts?

At lunch-time she dropped in at the beauty salon. Madame June hadn't come back yet, Madame Claire told her. She leant across the counter to whisper, 'Sometimes I think your sister is a very sick woman. But she keeps going; her courage is marvellous.'

'I do wish she'd see a doctor,' Janet said.

Madame Claire nodded slowly. 'Maybe she's afraid to see a doctor.'

Janet left determined to talk the situation over with June. She *must* see a doctor. It didn't matter what Tim said. Her mother was in her middle forties, a dangerous illness might lie ahead of her. This childish prank of youth she was playing must be discouraged. To hell with Tim!

# 13

Janet was tired and heartsore when she returned to her bed-sitting-room at the Beekman Towers Hotel. It would be nice to talk to someone. There's no aloneness like being alone in a vast city.

She thought of Julian. She would tell him about her mother's illness, ask his advice. She knew it would be difficult for him to interfere. He wasn't over-friendly with Tim, but she liked him all the more for that. Herself, she detested Tim.

Julian happened to be in his apartment and accepted her invitation to cocktails in the Beekman Towers penthouse, which had been turned into one huge glassed-in bar. She felt a thrill of pleasure seeing his tall loose-jointed frame striding through the tables towards her. She had never felt quite so close to him before.

He took his seat facing her. She asked him if he would have a dry martini. ‘This is my hotel. I’m host today,’ she reminded him, smiling.

‘Can I have a bourbon on the rocks? I’ve had a pretty rough day,’ he said. ‘What’s happened to the boy friend Mark? Has he deserted you?’

‘Mark is busy. Coleen is flying back from Honolulu. Did you know that her emeralds — I believe they were the famous Cameron Emeralds — were stolen last night?’

Julian nodded briefly. ‘I knew. The safe was a master one to break, all sorts of modern gadgets attached. There’s only one man in this country I think could have done this job, and that’s Ben Swartz. I’m sorry if he’s a friend of your brother-in-law Tim, but I understand that Ben has been going straight since he came out from prison. I saw them all the other evening at the Stork Club — Horace Greenslip, Reggie Fallow and Ben Swartz. Not a pretty combination when you include Master Tim.’

She said urgently, because she couldn't get those words of Tim's out of her mind, the words he had uttered upon entering the apartment, 'Tim said it had been child's play. But what had been child's play?'

He looked at her closely, almost as if he read what was passing through her mind. 'What do you know, if anything, Janet?'

'Nothing,' she assured him. 'Nothing. It was just a remark of Tim's when he came into the penthouse flat last night — something about it all being child's play. But he could have meant anything.'

'He could,' Julian replied grimly. 'But my advice to you is to stay out of this, Janet. Have as little to do with Tim Warren as you can. If he thought you knew or suspected anything, it would be dangerous for you. It might cost you your life.'

Janet was shaken. 'But Tim wouldn't harm me in any way.'

'Wouldn't he?' Julian raised one

untidy black eyebrow. 'My bet is he resents your presence. He might think you have too much influence over your sister. He might think she'd tell you something when you were alone.'

'But what could she tell me?' Janet stammered.

'I don't know. My theory is that Tim Warren is mixed up in some pretty shady business. That's why he hasn't made you more welcome at the flat. He hasn't made you very welcome, has he?'

'No,' she agreed. She added, 'I'm very worried about my sister. She ought to see a doctor, but Tim won't hear of it. I think she's pretty sick.'

'Then why aren't you down with her tonight?'

'Tim didn't make me feel very welcome yesterday,' she said. 'I might drop in later. Yes, I think I should drop in later.'

'Why don't we have dinner in Greenwich Village and then you can look in on your sister and I'll wait on in the restaurant?'

'Oh, could we do that?' Her voice was a small gasp of relief. 'I won't be long — not more than ten minutes or so. But I would like to assure myself that my sister is all right.'

'It's a date,' he said.

She looked up at him smiling, but there were tears behind the smile. 'You're very good to me, Julian. So very considerate.'

'I happen to like you,' he said gravely. 'I think I once mentioned I was in love with you. What's the use of having someone in love with you if you don't make use of them?'

'But it's so unfair to you.'

'I'll take the chance,' he said. 'Even though you only call me up when Mark is otherwise engaged.'

'It isn't very fair to you,' she said again.

'I love it,' he said. 'I love any chance of being with you.'

They finished their drinks and then he took her down in a taxi cab to Greenwich Village. It was always gay down there at night — the bars packed, the restaurants crowded. It was like the Chelsea of London, the King's Cross of Sydney.

They went down the basement steps into an Italian restaurant. There was an air of conviviality. Bottles of Chianti were on the tables, great dishes of spaghetti, ravioli and *tagliatelle* before the customers. They dined in candle-light and the waiters sang Italian songs as they served the food.

Janet was enchanted with the whole atmosphere of the place. It was so different from anything she had seen up till now.

'The Village, in its heyday, before the tourists discovered it, was quite some place,' Julian remarked. 'They used to hold art exhibitions in Washington Square. I believe they still do. But in the old days all the apartments were full of artists, song-writers, would-be drama-tists and novelists. Now many of the old buildings have been rebuilt. The pent-house apartment your sister lives in is an example. Do you want to eat first or do you want to go round and see her?'

'I'd like to go round and see her, if you don't mind,' Janet said. 'Then I could enjoy my dinner with an easy conscience. I'm still terribly worried about her health.'

'Do you want me to come round with you to the apartment door? I won't come in. I gather I'm not very welcome.'

'No, please don't come. It's quite near here. If you don't mind. I'd rather they didn't know I was out with you.'

'Just as you say. I'll order a bottle of Chianti and sip it while I'm waiting for you. Don't be gone too long.'

She grinned wryly. 'If Tim is home, I gather I'm not sufficiently welcome to stay too long.'

The block of apartment buildings was just around the corner. She didn't announce herself but entered the elevator and went up to the penthouse. She crossed the small dark garden with its boxed flowers and pressed the doorbell, which rang rhythmically. There was a pause before the door was opened. It was Tim.

'Oh, hello,' he said. His voice wasn't in the least welcoming. 'We didn't expect you down here tonight, Janet.'

'I was dining in the village and came round to ask how June was. May I come in?'

For a moment she thought he would bar her way.

'All right, come in,' he said gruffly. 'I've some friends here. June is in the bedroom, but there's no need to worry about her. She's considerably better.'

Ben Swartz and Horace Greenslip were with him. She bowed to them both and went towards the bedroom.

June looked a little better than she had looked on the previous day, but she saw at once that she had been crying.

'Tim wants me to go away for a holiday,' she said. 'He said we both need a break. But I don't want to leave you, Janet. Not after I've just met you again. It's meant more to me re-meeting you than anything I can say.'

Janet touched her hand softly. 'Mother.'

Her mother withdrew her hand sharply. 'Don't. Don't say that here,' she whispered urgently. 'Tim might overhear.'

'He's with some friends of his in the lounge.'

'I know. They have a business deal on. He never wants me there when he's talking business.'

'I think you should see a doctor, June.'

But again her mother shook her head violently. 'I'll be all right. Tim says I'll be all right directly we get away. If Tim didn't agree, I wouldn't dare call in a doctor, Janet.'

'But you must if your health — why your very life — may be at stake.'

'Oh, I'll be all right,' June said as cheerfully as possible. 'I have these little turns. I get over them as quickly as anything. I'll be up at the beauty parlour tomorrow.'

'I'm dining with someone in the

Village,' Janet told her 'I thought I'd take the opportunity to drop in.'

'Thanks, darling.' Her mother clutched her hands, almost clawing them. 'You don't know what a comfort you are to me, how pleased I am that you're over here. But you'd better go now. Your boy friend may be waiting, and besides, Tim — Tim may want to get on with the business he's discussing with his friends.'

She had to re-pass through the lounge. She saw that Reggie Fallow had joined their number. The four of them sat with their heads together in earnest conversation, but the conversation was scarcely above a whisper.

Tim saw her coming and sprang to his feet. 'As you see, June's much better, isn't she, Janet? I'm thinking of taking her away on a little holiday. Do her the world of good — better than all the medicines the doctors prescribe.' He laughed his buoyant healthy laugh and added, 'I have no faith in doctors.'

You're so damn' healthy you've never

needed one, she thought.

'I'm taking care of June.' In a lower voice he added, 'She's my wife. She belongs to me.'

He didn't ask her to drop by again. She knew by this time Tim hated her as much as she hated him. But to hell with him, she thought; she wasn't going to allow him to separate her from her mother, especially now when she thought her mother needed her. She was in a somewhat disquietened mood when she returned to the restaurant.

'Don't look so glum,' Julian said. 'What happened? Is your sister any worse?'

She shook her head. 'She seems a little better. Tim's talking about taking her away on a trip.'

She noticed his attention quicken. 'Tim Warren is going away on a trip?'

She nodded. 'He thinks it would do June more good than all the doctors' prescriptions. But I don't feel right about it somehow. I still wish she'd see a doctor.'

'Were they alone together in the apartment?' Julian asked.

'Those three friends of his — they always stick around him — were with him.'

'Do you mean Horace Greenslip, Reggie Fallow and Ben Swartz?'

She nodded.

'You didn't happen to overhear anything they said?' His voice was sharp again, excited.

'No. When I came back into the room they were talking together in whispers. Tim doesn't like me, Julian. It makes it awfully awkward for June and me.'

He took her hand and held it gently. He said in a low grave voice, 'June is your mother. You don't mind my knowing, Janet?'

She started, her face went very white. 'How did you know?' she whispered.

'Merely by putting two and two together. Despite her dyed hair and all her face-lifts, June is considerably older than you — old enough to be your mother. You're strongly pulled towards her. More strongly than you would be to a sister whom you haven't seen for eleven years. You're very alike in many ways; your mannerisms, your gestures. Do you remember I said that to you in Sydney?'

'I haven't forgotten.' Her voice was ragged. 'It's a ridiculous situation.'

After a pause, he said, 'It's all Tim Warren's doing, isn't it? I sensed he became infatuated with your mother as many young men do with older women, though I can't imagine how he persuaded her to elope with him. But elope with him she did. He is too vain to have people think he is married to a much older woman. I bet he insisted on the deception under threat that your mother must never correspond with you again. She couldn't bear the thought of that. She had to keep some kind of contact with you. She agreed to the elder sister suggestion. Poor woman. There was nothing else for her to do.'

'But why couldn't she have stood up to Tim?'

‘I’m afraid she’s got Tim in her blood,’ he said seriously. ‘She dotes upon him. A separation from him would mean death to her. She was willing to carry on with the ridiculous situation. After all, she felt it was better than nothing.’

‘You don’t despise her, Julian?’

‘No. Why should I? She was pushed up against the wall. I’d say she had no alternative. I have nothing but pity for her.’

‘Did you know anything of all this when you advised me not to come to New York?’

‘I knew enough about Tim Warren not to want any girl I even liked associating with him,’ he said. ‘I was sorry for you with your rosy dreams, my darling.’

‘You were right in both things,’ she said slowly. ‘Tim is objectionable. He is trying to dissociate me from June. I’m sure that’s the reason of this proposed trip. And as for Mark’ — she hesitated and shrugged — ‘he’s all set on meeting Coleen.’

'But you still don't think he's in love with her?'

She hesitated, twisting her fork round the spaghetti on her plate. 'I think she has a certain hold on him. A very definite hold. But I hope, I pray, that Mark isn't in love with her.'

'You want me to hope so, too?' he asked, looking across at her rather sourly.

'Julian.' She touched his hand. 'You promised to be my friend. You promised to help me if you could in gaining Mark's love.'

'When are you going to see him again?'

'He suggested that we drive down to Ridgefield in Connecticut for the week-end and that he introduces me to his parents. I do hope it will come off. I'd like that more than anything in this world.'

'I'll see if I can get Coleen tied up in town with police inquiries over the missing emeralds,' he said.

She stared at him. 'You could do that, Julian?'

'I have a little influence with the police,' he said shortly. His tone of voice discouraged her from asking further questions.

But she persisted. 'Julian,' she whispered. 'Are you that man so popular in the films and on TV — a private eye?'

He shook his head and laughed. 'I'm not a private eye. Sorry to disappoint you, Janet. But now and again I'm able to give the police a tip or two that comes off. I'm sure they'll co-operate with me in this. Have your week-end in Ridgefield with Mark. Blast you,' he said, and then he added, 'darling.'

She was able to shake off a few of her worries over dinner. It was an excellent dinner. Following the spaghetti was veal cutlets Bolognaise cooked with cheese and baby mushrooms. Afterwards they had coffee and Strega.

She said, before she said good night to him, 'I'm glad you know, Julian. It helps a lot to share a secret with another.'

'Are you going to tell Mark?'

She shook her head. 'I couldn't. It would make me look a fool. It is really an absurd situation.'

'But he'll have to know about your mother if and when you marry him.'

She laughed a little shakily. 'Mark and I are still a long way from marriage. He has an affection for me, I know, but how much further than that it goes, I don't know.'

'Good luck to you anyhow for the week-end,' he said. 'I'll keep my promise: I'll use all my influence to keep Coleen busy at police headquarters.'

But she still only half believed he could accomplish that.

# 14

'Here we are, Janet.'

Mark drew the car up before the gates of a large, attractive old Colonial home in Ridgefield. There was a tennis court and flowering gardens. He opened the drive gates and drove the car up to the front door.

'This house is old Colonial,' he told her. 'And Mum and Dad have furnished it with perfect antique pieces.'

A coloured butler came out of the door across the porch and down the front steps. 'Welcome home, Mister Mark,' he said. 'This sure is some day.'

'Yes, this sure is some day. This is Miss Freeman, Louis. She's come all the way from Australia to work with me in the office.'

'I welcome you, ma'am,' Louis said, bowing to her gravely. 'Shall I take the bags inside, Mister Mark?'

'Please do,' he said. 'And where are Mother and Father?'

'Your father's in his study, Mister Mark. And your mother is upstairs resting. But she'll be down soon enough when she hears that you have come home at last. The master, Mr. Dexter, has been wondering too, how soon you would be getting here.'

Mark laughed his pleasant easy laugh. 'Come along inside, Janet. We'll rout out my parents.'

But as they passed down the hallway an elderly man appeared. He was tall and very thin. He had grey hair, which he wore rather long and the same steel-grey eyes that Mark had.

'This is my father, Mr. Fabian Dexter — Janet Freeman,' Mark introduced them. 'She's a pretty plucky kid, Father. She's come all the way from her home town, Sydney, to edit some manuscripts for me.'

'You're very welcome.' Mr. Dexter gave a courtly little bow. 'You must tell me all about Australia. It's a country which has always fascinated me.'

She laughed. 'Well, we don't have kangaroos hopping about the streets, or koala bears living up in our trees any longer.'

'I didn't think you had.' He smiled. 'It's a great wool-growing country, isn't it — one of the most important wool countries in this world — I believe they call the ranches stations. Have you ever lived on a station, Janet? I may call you Janet? We Americans are informal, as you know.'

'Please call me Janet. And although I've visited a station, I've never lived on one. I've always lived in Sydney.'

He called up the stairs: 'Edith, are you there? Mark has arrived with his guest.'

'I'm coming, Fabian. I'm coming straight away. It's just that I hadn't expected them so soon with all this Saturday traffic.'

She appeared almost within the instant on the top of the stairs, a small rather faded pretty woman, with brown hair turning grey and large brown eyes. She ran quickly down the stairs and clasped both of Janet's hands. 'Welcome, my dear. Welcome to the States. Mark has written us about you, what a wonderful help you were to him in Sydney and how kind you were to him besides. We want to make you especially welcome here in the old homestead.'

Janet smiled back at her warmly and said, 'I already feel very welcome.'

'Would you like to go up to your room first, my dear, and then we'll have some tea? I'm sure you'll like tea, being an Australian. Our men mainly prefer highballs at tea-time.'

'Please don't worry about me,' Janet said. 'I should hate you to get tea specially for me.'

'But you must be tired after your journey,' Mrs. Dexter said. 'We'll go upstairs first to your room and then Louis will bring tea into the lounge. I hope you'll find enough in the way of enjoyment down here, Miss Freeman. Mr. Dexter and I lead very quiet lives.'

Janet laughed. 'I seem to have been living like a spinning top ever since I left Sydney. I shall love a few days' rest and relaxation. But please call me Janet.'

'Carry — she's the coloured maid — will unpack for you,' Mrs. Dexter said. 'Would you like to go and wash your hands?' She led Janet into a bathroom that adjoined the bedroom. 'I'll meet you downstairs in the lounge,' she added.

They were charming people. Janet was keeping her fingers crossed. They both seemed to like her. But would they like her so much when they knew how she felt towards their only son, Mark? But essentially they seemed well-bred simple people, very different from the Café Society crowd that both Coleen and Mark patronised in New York. But she was glad he had brought her down to meet his people. It made her feel much closer to him, as though she wasn't merely an office assistant but a girl of importance in his life.

The four of them dined alone, but some friends of theirs came in afterwards. There was talk, and drinks were circulated.

'What do you hear of Coleen Hausman?' his mother asked Mark. 'Have you seen her recently?'

So she didn't know that Coleen had met Mark in Honolulu?

'Didn't you read about her emeralds — the famous Cameron Emeralds — being stolen?' Mark asked quickly.

'I think I did read something about it,' his mother said. 'She prized those emeralds greatly, I believe. Poor child, she has always been unfortunate ever since she was in her teens.'

'I shouldn't say that Coleen has exactly been unforunate, Mother,' Mark said, a little dryly.

'But yes,' his mother said. 'She ran off with that young writer fellow. I understood from her parents the marriage was on the rocks even before he got himself killed in a car crash. I understand it would ultimately have ended in divorce. Ever since then when I've seen her, she's been such a restless creature. She never seems to know what she wants. But then even as a child and a growing girl, she always had that hypersensitive restless nature. I shouldn't think she could settle down to anything or any man.' She laughed and patted Mark on the hand. 'You were childhood sweethearts. I can't tell you how relieved I was when she eventually eloped with Henry Hausman.'

'I can't say that I was relieved, Mother,' Mark said with some bitterness. 'It was a sad blow to my young pride.'

'But you've got over it,' his mother said cheerfully. 'And now you and Coleen are the best of friends. Have you met Coleen, Janet?'

'Yes, I've met her,' Janet said briefly, and added, as though she felt that was inadequate, 'She is very lovely.'

'A most beautiful woman,' Mark's mother agreed. 'But I can't see her mothering a growing family, somehow. She would be always flitting off to some odd corner of the earth.'

She left them then, to talk to some of her other guests.

'Mother is old-fashioned,' Mark said. 'She wouldn't have approved of Coleen meeting me in Honolulu.'

'How is Coleen taking the theft of her emeralds, Mark?' Janet inquired.

'She's all out to get them back and have the thieves put where they ought to be — behind iron bars. She says if she doesn't get results quickly enough from the police, she'll hire a private eye. I told her the police are always your best bet. Anyhow she's going to offer a reward.'

'She didn't mind your coming away this week-end, Mark?'

He grimaced. 'She didn't like it. Apparently she's tied up with interviews at headquarters. She thought I ought to stick by her.'

'Does she know I'm here with you, Mark?'

He looked embarrassed. He ran a hand back over his hair. 'To be quite frank, she doesn't. Coleen can be jealous and possessive as the devil. I thought it wiser not to mention it.'

Another couple came over to speak to them. Janet was secretly dismayed. Hadn't he the strength of character to tell Coleen he was bringing her, Janet, down for the week-end to stay with his parents? But how came it she was tied up with those interviews at headquarters? Had Julian arranged it? But that didn't seem possible. He had said he wasn't a private eye. Then what had he to do with the police?

They went to bed conventionally early — early for New York, with its streaming lights and neon signs which remain lighted until sunrise.

* * *

The following morning his father and mother were going to church, but Mark suggested that instead Janet and he should go for a long tramp across country.

'I want to show her the New England countryside,' he said. 'Perhaps you'd have a few sandwiches cut for us, Mum? We'll take a picnic lunch. We'll be back early.'

Janet saw that his mother was loath to have him go. Living here in Ridgefield she must see very little of her only son. Perhaps Janet should have suggested that Mark and she should stay with them, but she was so eager for this tramp and picnic together.

They set off across country. The New England scene was a riot of all colours. They passed stately mansions and cottages, but soon they were off into the forest. They decided to stop and have their lunch by a small stream that gurgled over stones. They spread the luncheon hamper out. There was much more than sandwiches: cold chicken, ham and tongue, bottled fruit and cream, and a bottle of white wine which they cooled off in the stream. The leaves of the lower branches of the tree flopped low over their heads; the grass was green but dry, there was here and there a clump of wild flowers. It was the perfect setting for a picnic. New York might have been a million miles away.

They ate and drank the wine and then they relaxed. He laid his head upon her lap. 'Do you mind, darling?' he asked. 'I feel so blissfully happy.'

She stroked his dark brown hair, twisting little locks of it about her fingers.

'Like it here, darling?' he asked. 'I mean not only here but in New York?'

'I like it especially here,' she said. 'At this minute. But seriously, I'll never be able to thank you enough for all you have done for me, Mark.'

'You'll remember me in your heart when you go back to Sydney?' he said. 'That is, if you do have to go back to Sydney.'

'I suppose I shall have to, once my six months is up.'

'You could always go across the

border and re-enter with a fresh permit.' He reached up one of his hands and clasped one of her wrists. 'I don't want to lose you, Janet.'

She whispered, 'I don't want to lose you either, Mark.'

'I never thought I'd want to marry anyone, but it's conceivable, just conceivable, I might want to marry you, Janet. In time, I mean. We've got to find out a great deal more about each other.'

'I thought we knew a good deal already about each other, Mark.'

'Some things,' he agreed. He twisted restlessly and observed, 'I wish like hell that Coleen had never come back from Honolulu.'

'Does Coleen Hausman worry you very much, Mark?'

'Somewhat,' he admitted, biting his lower lip. 'More than somewhat, perhaps. She says she's very much in love with me — has been for years. Even before poor Henry crashed himself in a car. She said her elopement with Henry was sheer madness. It was because I had started a slight flirtation with another girl. Damn it all, I've even forgotten her name. Coleen's beautiful; she's all a man might want in a woman, but I don't wholly trust her. I mean I don't trust that if some other man came along, she wouldn't go all out for him and leave me in the lurch again.'

Janet's heart felt sick inside her. 'Then you really do care for her, Mark?'

'Oh, yes. Throughout everything I've always been in love with Coleen,' he said. 'Not that I've wanted to be in love with her — far from it. That's one reason I asked you to come over here. We got on so well together in Sydney; you even made me forget Coleen for a time. I know you're the sort of girl I ought to marry, Janet, the sort of girl who would make my people happy.'

She leant further over him. 'And you, Mark; could I make you happy?'

He raised himself and putting his arms about her, he held her closely to him and kissed her. 'I want you to be the girl who will make me happy, Janet.

I want that more than anything in this world.'

Everything they might have said would have been an anti-climax after that. They repacked the picnic basket and started homewards.

'In the meantime we'll be friends, eh, Janet?' he said finally. 'Very close friends, my darling. I like everything about you, the buoyant way you walk, your longish auburn hair — and please don't have it cut again, will you, darling? — your bright hazel eyes which seem to hold a world of dreams. I told you I thought I was falling in love with you. I do seriously believe I am.'

They walked home hand in hand like two children. The trees were very green, the sky was very blue above. It was a perfect day, perfect day.

They had tea with his parents. Afterwards his father took Mark into the study and Janet was left alone with his mother. She asked her numerous questions about herself, about her childhood, her father the professor, and about her mother. Janet found that difficult to answer. She said she had lost her mother when she was eleven years old, and Mrs. Dexter seemed to take it for granted that her mother had passed on. What would she think of the present set-up, the ridiculous sister relationship? She said she had a sister in New York, who owned a beauty parlour.

'I hope Mark will marry. I should like to have the pleasure of grandchildren before I die. But Coleen Hausman, as she was then, has always been in his blood. He didn't easily get over the affair. But I hope he has got over it now. I hope most sincerely so. Try to help him Janet.'

They had a cold supper presently and afterwards went soon to bed, as they had to make an early start for New York in the morning. Janet had been very happy over this week-end. Her hopes were high.

The journey back to New York along the wide highways was speedy and pleasant. Mark dropped Janet at Beekman Towers Hotel to change her dress before she came up to the office.

'Enjoyed it, darling?'

'Oh, so much . . . so much.'

He raised her lips to his and kissed them. 'I enjoyed it, too,' he said.

# 15

At lunchtime she called in to the beauty salon to see if her mother was back at work. Mary Claire shook her head. 'She hasn't been near the salon for several days. I wonder if I might speak to you alone, Miss Freeman?'

Mystified, Janet followed her into one of the cubicles.

'It's very strange,' she said. 'We've had no communication at all from your sister. Of course we're all carrying on as usual. But this morning there were several men in the store. They indicated that Madame June's beauty business was up for sale. I don't know what to think.' She wrung her hands together. 'Surely if she intended to sell out, I would have been one of the first persons to know.'

Janet couldn't in any way be helpful to the deeply distressed Mary Claire.

She could only promise to try and see her mother that evening and find out what was happening.

On an impulse she called Julian. She had to try his number several times before she found him at home.

'Everything go well over the weekend?' he asked.

'It was lovely.'

'Did Mark ask you to marry him?'

She hesitated. 'No, he didn't exactly ask me to marry him, but we talked of marriage.'

'I don't say I wish you luck with him. I want you for myself, Janet.'

'But you promised to help me with Mark.'

'That was some time ago before I had fallen so deeply in love with you myself.'

She flushed. 'Oh, Julian, I wish I had you near me. I wish we weren't so far apart, a whole section of New York between us.'

'Will you dine with me tonight?'

'I could,' she said. 'But I have to drop

in at June's first. She hasn't been near the beauty salon. There's a rumour that it's up for sale.'

'You don't say!' His voice was immediately on the alert. 'I'd like to know more about this sale. Your mother didn't say anything to you about it last time you saw her?'

It seemed natural for Julian to call June her mother now.

'No, she didn't.'

'Let's dine in the Village. There's a very good French restaurant I know of where they serve the famous *coq au vin*. It's not far from your mother's apartment. But then everything in the Village is very close. We'll go there, have a glass of wine, and then I'll wait for you as I did the other time. Shall we say six o'clock? I'm going to be pretty busy until then.'

It was pleasant, the thought of dining with Julian. Mark had said he thought he was falling in love with her; he had even said she was the type of girl he thought he should marry. But it was a relief to have Julian say right out he loved her and wanted to marry her. She was a little tired of Mark's indecisions. She still believed she loved him, but she was beginning to wonder if she loved him enough. Even if she eventually succeeded in marrying him, would Coleen always be the ghost-figure in her life — the woman he had loved in his teens, the woman she suspected he loved even now? It hurt to admit that, but she had to admit it. She wondered if there was always another woman in a man's life somewhere?

She shook herself mentally and got back to her work. This novel she was reading now was a pleasant novel of Sydney life centred around Vaucluse, Point Piper and Darling Point. It was very well written, but she wondered if it would be attractive to an American audience.

That evening, while Julian waited for her in the French restaurant, she went round to her mother's apartment. Tim opened the door to her. He scowled when he saw her. His usual charm was completely lacking.

'What do you want, Janet?' he asked bluntly.

'I want to see June,' Janet said.

'I'm afraid you can't see her. I won't have her upset in any way.'

'But why should I upset her?'

'You always upset her. You remind her too much of the past. I want you to keep clear of this apartment, Janet. I didn't want you to come over to the States.'

'I know that,' she said quietly. 'But all the same I insist upon seeing my mother.'

'And I refuse to let her see you. After all, I'm her legal husband. As I told you, she isn't well enough to see anyone.'

'Has she seen a doctor yet?'

'That's my business,' he said curtly. 'Now get out!' He slammed the door in her face.

She stood there, wondering what on earth she should do. She had no means of forcing an entrance. Besides, Tim would as likely as not throw her out bodily.

She went back to the small French restaurant where she had left Julian. She was in such a state of distress she was almost in tears.

He looked at her with deep concern. He leant across the table: 'Well, did you see your mother?'

She shook her head. She bit her lower lip. 'Tim wouldn't let me inside the apartment. He told me to keep clear of the penthouse in future. He wouldn't even tell me if he had had a doctor see my mother.'

Julian said, 'I'll go round with you afterwards, if you like. We'll force him to let you see her. Tim may be a mass of phoney charm, but he has no strength in his muscles. I'm not afraid to tackle him.'

'Do you think I should go round again?' Janet said. Her voice was tense and very much on edge.

'If it will relieve your mind, I'll take

you round. But first let's have some dinner. Even though you may have no appetite, try to eat something.'

The *coq au vin*, the speciality of the place, was very appetising, but she had little taste for it. She couldn't get over Tim's rudeness to her and his blunt refusal to let her see her mother. He had as good as told her she wasn't wanted around there any longer. But what was happening? Why was the business being sold? How ill really was her mother?

Julian tried to make conversation. He asked her about the week-end.

'Mark's parents are very nice,' she said. 'His mother seemed to like me. But I can't think or talk about it now. I can think of nothing but my mother.'

He patted her hand. 'Poor kid. I'd do anything for you in this world, Janet, you know that. I think Tim's a coward at heart. If I go round with you, you might be able to see your mother.'

He insisted she drink some Burgundy to keep her spirits up. They had strong black coffee afterwards.

'When you're ready, we'll go. You know I love you. I don't just think I love you — I really do. I'd marry you tomorrow in the City Hall if you'd have me.'

'I like you very much, Julian. Perhaps I more than like you,' she whispered.

'But you can't make up your mind between us — that's it, isn't it? Mark has all the glamour. But he also has Coleen. She's not going to lose hold of him in a hurry.'

She took another drink of wine. She felt she needed it to sustain her courage. 'If you really mean you'll come with me, Julian, we'll go round now.'

'I'll come. I'm not afraid of Master Tim.'

But it took her not a little courage to enter that apartment building again, to press the elevator button and go up to the twentieth floor. They crossed the garden and rang the rhythmical chimes on the bell.

Tim opened the door. 'What the

devil are you two doing here,' he demanded.

Julian's face looked very grim, his voice was hard, as he said, 'Janet wants to see her mother. Oh, yes, I know she is her mother, Tim. Your stupid little pretence didn't deceive me for a moment. Will you let her in quietly or must I make you let her in?'

'I refuse.' Tim started to close the door in their faces, but Julian quickly inserted his foot and pressed his hard lean frame down on Tim's softer one.

'Do you want a fight, Tim? I'm quite prepared.'

Tim's fist bashed out. 'I've told you to get the hell out of my apartment.'

Julian neatly parried the blow and gave Tim a punch in his stomach, which doubled him up on the floor in pain.

'I'll watch over him,' he said to Janet. 'Scoot down the corridor and see your mother.'

Her mother was still in bed. She looked very grey, very worn. 'What's happening?' she whispered.

'I had to come in and see you,' Janet said. 'I came earlier but Tim wouldn't let me come into the apartment.'

'Tim's jealous of you, fearfully jealous.'

'Have you seen a doctor?' Janet demanded.

'No. But I'll be all right. I'll be all right tomorrow, Janet. But who's with you?'

'Julian Gaden.'

'Tim hates him. Why did you bring him here?'

'Tim wouldn't have let me in otherwise. Is it true you're going to sell the beauty parlour?'

'Tim's going to sell it; the business is in his name. But please go now, Janet. Please go.' She was crying and wringing her hands together. 'I'm afraid. I'm so dreadfully afraid.'

'What are you afraid of?' Janet asked gently.

'I'm afraid that Tim will clear off and leave me,' June whispered. 'When I'm ill, I look so very old. The doctors may order me into a sanatorium and then I'd have no hold over him. I think he will clear out of the country.'

'Will you ring me up at the Beekman Towers Hotel early tomorrow morning or at the East-West Publishing office in the daytime and let me know how you are?' Janet pleaded.

'I'll do that. I promise, Janet. But go quickly now. Go quickly.'

Tim was just recovering from the blow, but he was still in pain. Julian stood over him, every muscle taut.

'I'll get back on you for this,' Tim growled. 'I'll get back on you both, forcing your way in here, assaulting me. I'll call in the police.'

'But that's the last thing you want to do, isn't it Tim?' Julian said in a low, quiet voice. 'You're not anxious to be mixed up with the police in any way, are you?'

'Oh, get the hell out of here,' Tim said morosely. 'Janet has satisfied herself that June is still alive.'

'I want you to promise me you'll

send for a doctor,' she said. 'Otherwise I'm not going to leave you and my mother alone, Tim.'

'Maybe if I think a doctor is necessary, I'll send for one,' he said in a surly voice, hugging his abdomen. 'But neither of us wants you around here.'

'I'll only be satisfied when I know that a doctor has been to see my mother,' Janet said.

'All right, I give in. I'll get in touch with a doctor,' Tim said unexpectedly. 'I know a good one in the Village. If you both clear out of here, I'll telephone him now.'

Julian looked towards Janet. 'What do you say?'

'I'd rather wait until Tim makes the call,' Janet said.

'You make the call,' Julian said to Tim. 'Or do you want me to belt the daylights out of you again?'

Suddenly, Tim rose to his feet, limped towards the telephone and made a call to a Doctor Barnett. 'June won't thank you if he insists she go to hospital,' he said. 'That's the one place she doesn't want to go.'

'Maybe he won't insist on that,' Janet said. 'But I'd like to wait here until he comes.'

'You'd stick around when you know you're not welcome?' Tim blustered.

'Did you hear what the lady said, Tim?' Julian said. He seemed to flex his muscles as though preparing for another bout.

Tim gave in. But then Julian had said he was a coward.

Janet left the two men in the lounge. She went back into the bedroom to see her mother. 'It's all right, darling,' she said, stroking her mother's head. 'A doctor is coming. Tim telephoned for one.'

'Tim telephoned for one?' Her mother's voice was startled. 'But he hasn't wanted me to see a doctor — not for several weeks at least. I told you he hates it when I'm sick. Don't do anything to upset Tim, please, Janet. Lately he's been under a very heavy strain. I don't know what it is. He won't tell me. But he says we have to sell the salon and get clear of the country as soon as possible. He's talking about going down to South America. He says I must be well enough to come or else he'll have to leave me behind.' She wept again.

Janet did her best to comfort her.

They were lucky that the doctor arrived almost immediately. Janet left the bedroom while he examined her mother.

He came out, his face looking very grave. 'I'm afraid I'll have to send Mrs. Warren to hospital at once,' he said. 'She must have an immediate operation. If you like, Mr. Warren, I'll telephone through to several hospitals I know of and see if they can find her a bed.'

Tim looked warily at Julian, then he nodded. 'Yes, do that.'

'I'd better stay with your wife until the ambulance comes, Mr. Warren. Her condition is very serious indeed,' the doctor said.

'What hospital are you sending her to?' Janet asked.

'St. Luke's Hospital in East Sixtieth Street,' he said. 'But I don't think she'll be fit enough to see visitors for some few days.'

'But I can telephone?' Janet said.

The ambulance arrived shortly afterwards. Janet packed June's bag. She was weeping uncontrollably. 'I'll lose Tim,' she sobbed. 'Timmy will go away to South America and forget all about me.'

Janet tried to soothe her. 'I'm sure he wouldn't do such a thing.'

Her mother moaned and said, 'Tim is ruthless. But I love him so.'

Janet bent her head. It was queer how some completely worthless man could keep a woman fascinated and in love with him for years.

After the ambulance men had gone, Julian and Janet left the apartment. The doctor said good-bye to Tim, but Julian and Janet didn't say a word. Julian took the doctor aside in the foyer and had a few words with him. When he rejoined Janet, he put his arm through hers. He said they would take a taxi back to the Beekman Towers Hotel. He was very gentle with her.

They didn't speak much during the taxi ride back. The presence of the driver prevented them. Julian's face was grim and Janet was white-faced and terrified.

'I think a good stiff drink is indicated after all that,' Julian said.

He took her straight up to the bar at the top of the Beekman Towers Hotel. He didn't ask her what she wanted, but ordered her a bourbon on the rocks. 'Drink it down straight off,' he told her. 'And that's an order.'

She did as he said. The drink sent a rush of warm blood coursing through her.

'What did the doctor say? Is the news so very bad, Julian?'

He took both her hands and held them tightly. His voice was slightly hoarse. 'Pretty bad,' he said. 'She has an advanced cancerous growth in her lung. It ought to have been operated on months ago, even a year or more ago.'

Her voice shook and broke: 'Does he hold out much hope?'

'You've got to be brave, Janet. I'm afraid there's very little hope.'

'Excuse me,' she said. 'Good-bye and thank you for all you've done, Julian.' The tears were coursing down her cheeks.

He got to his feet. 'I'll see you to your room. I'll come back and settle the bill afterwards.'

He took her to the door. She opened it. He came in after her. 'Janet, my dearest girl, I am so very sorry for you.'

She leant her head against his chest and wept unrestrainedly.

'My darling, darling girl.' He stroked her hair. He kissed her cheek. 'Do you want me to go? Or am I any comfort to you?'

'Please stay with me, Julian,' she whispered. 'I know you are my friend. It seems too tragic to think that she and I should have met again after so many years and that at the time she was practically dying of cancer. How I hate Tim Warren. She was afraid to see a doctor. I suppose she was afraid he would tell her the truth, and Tim couldn't bear an invalid around. It had become a thing with her not to see a doctor. She couldn't help what she did in the past, in the present. Tim is an obsession with her.'

'You are an obsession with me, darling,' Julian said, stroking her face. 'I wish I could leave you with some hope. But the doctor seemed to think there was very little hope. Maybe in the end it is for the best, my darling. I can't explain.'

'She's so afraid that Tim will go to South America and leave her.'

'Tim won't go to South America.' Julian's voice was harsh. It grated.

# 16

June never recovered from the operation, which in some ways was as well. Tim Warren was arrested that same night in his apartment for being concerned in the theft of Coleen Hausman's emeralds and other New York jewel robberies. The fence who had bought the Cameron Emeralds found them too hot to handle. When the search got very intense he had thrown in his hand and gone to the police. Ben Swartz was arrested too. He broke under the third degree and implicated Reggie Fallow, Horace Greenslip and Tim Warren.

Tim had apparently planned the job. He got to know the layout of the fashionable New York houses when he sent the girls from the beauty salon into their homes. June had sometimes gone herself. She had obviously given him valuable information. Ben Swartz had cracked the safe.

Coleen Hausman got her priceless set of emeralds back.

Janet told Mark that her sister had died on the operating table. He urged her to take a few days off. She was grateful. She was heartbroken about her mother's death, and yet as Julian had said, it might be for the best. Her mother had undoubtedly been involved in the robberies. She pitied her mother tremendously and loved her. But she was too weak where Tim was concerned. As she grew older she would probably never have held him. Perhaps her death had been merciful.

Janet went for long walks around New York by herself. Sometimes Julian accompanied her. He took her to the various art galleries and museums. He showed her Wall Street and the famous aquarium. He was all gentleness and kindness. She wondered she had ever thought him brusque and overbearing. His was a hard face, but a strong face.

In the days which followed she came to depend upon him more and more.

Mark seemed almost a stranger when finally she returned to the office. He hadn't tried to contact her in the meantime. 'I thought you would prefer to be alone with your grief,' he said.

She smiled faintly. 'I wasn't entirely alone, Mark.'

He didn't question her as to whom she was with, and she was glad. But she had learnt that you don't want to be alone with your sorrow; you want a sympathetic shoulder to lean on, a sympathetic mind to read your mind. In these past days Julian and she had grown very close to each other. It became increasingly difficult for her to visualise a life without his care and protection.

It was several weeks later when Mark invited her out to dinner. In the meantime he had been to Hollywood on a business trip in connection with the sale of one of the novels his firm was publishing. Apparently while he was there another book had come up for the studio's consideration and he had stayed out there to try and clinch the deal. Both deals had come off successfully and he was in high spirits when he returned to New York. But it was several days after his return that he invited Janet out to dinner.

'We'll have a quiet meal at Martinique's,' he told her. 'There's a great deal I have to discuss with you, Janet.'

She wore the dinner gown she had bought at Saks. It suited her. She had a little more colour in her cheeks now than she had had in the past weeks.

The Martinique Restaurant was in the East Sixties and was very smart. The head waiter escorted them to a side table. The décor was modern, slightly suggesting the Spanish style. A fountain played in the middle of the restaurant. Palms half screened their table.

'It must have been a great grief to you, your sister dying so shortly after you came over,' Mark said. 'But apparently she had been suffering for some time. She just refused to see a doctor.' He shook his head. 'Women can be very stubborn. Everyone is very pleased with your work at the office, Janet. I'm very pleased I brought you over; pleased in more ways than one. My mother continually asks about you in her letters. It seems you made a great hit with her.'

'She was very sweet to me. She's a charming woman.'

He laughed. 'I think so, anyway. Now let's concentrate on what we're going to eat. This place is celebrated for its steaks. What do you say to baked oysters and steak? They're recognised as having the best steaks in New York City here, and it's a town where steak usually makes the main course of a meal.'

'I know,' she said. 'But they're usually so large I can't get through half of one.'

'I'll order a small steak for you. Myself, I could face a man-size one. I was busy today; I lunched off sandwiches in the office. But I've a roaring appetite now.'

They discussed his trip to Hollywood while they dined. There was soft music in the background. He told her about the various studios, the movie stars he had met, the directors and the office people he had had to deal with.

'Hollywood is becoming increasingly difficult. In the old days if a novel was a fair seller it was more or less easy to get a sale. But now with TV competition they want only the most outstanding successes. An ordinary book, unless it is very well reviewed and chosen by the book societies, doesn't stand a chance.'

He mentioned the Brown Derby and some of the other Hollywood restaurants he had been to, including the famous Coconut Grove.

Finally, when coffee was served, his grey eyes held hers. 'Would you marry me, Janet?' he asked abruptly.

She was completely startled for a moment. Nothing had led up to this sudden proposal. She raised her hazel eyes to his. 'Why do you want to marry me, Mark?'

'There are a number of reasons I want to marry you,' he told her gravely. 'I think you'd be good for me. You'd be the sort of wife I should have; the sort of wife of whom my parents would approve. We have a great deal in common. You understand the publishing business. I think you understand me too, Janet.'

'You're not trying to escape, Mark?' she asked him quietly.

She saw him flush; his eyes left hers and fell towards the table. 'It may be a little of that as well,' he said. 'I'm convinced I'll never get Coleen completely out of my system until I'm married to someone else — you preferably.'

She was very still suddenly. 'Do you love me, Mark?'

His face paled visibly, his lips set in a tight line. 'Must I be completely honest, Janet?'

She nodded. 'Please, Mark. It's our only hope.'

'I love you,' he said. 'I'd love you

more if I could get Coleen out of my system. I loved you in Sydney; that's why I wanted to bring you back with me. But when she met us in Honolulu, everything seemed to go wrong. I — I have to admit she has a fascination for me. A very strong fascination. But I can't see us being happy together — not now, not in the future. That's why I'm asking you, I'm begging you, to take a chance and marry me, my darling.'

Her heart was beating fast. She had loved Mark; didn't she still love him? She must. One didn't change one's love overnight. And yet as she sat there she had a sudden vision of Julian, with his arresting-looking hard-featured face, his floppy black hair, his very blue eyes, the cleft in his chin and his grin — that diabolical grin of his. If he were listening in on this conversation, wouldn't he be grinning now?

She seemed to feel he was very close to her in that moment. 'I don't know, Mark,' she said finally. 'I'm honoured that you asked me to marry you, but I'd have to feel you were completely mine — only mine.'

He gave a slightly sour smile. 'It doesn't pay to be too honest, does it? Will you think over the proposition, Janet?'

She nodded. 'Yes, I'll think over it, Mark. After that night in Nadi in the Fijian Islands I loved you very much. Maybe I still love you just as much, but I feel confused. I don't want to say anything definite now. Will you, do you, understand?'

He nodded. 'Yes, I suppose I understand. But it isn't what I hoped for, Janet. How long will it take you to make up your mind?'

'I don't know,' she said. 'I think perhaps it's you who have to make up your own mind, Mark.'

'But I have asked you to marry me.'

'I know. But when I marry you, it mustn't be as an escape from anyone; it must be because you want me more than you want anything in this world.

I'm sorry, Mark.'

'But you haven't refused; you will think it over?' he insisted.

'Yes, I shall think it over.'

He took her home shortly afterwards.

'May I kiss you?' he said outside the door of her room. 'I swear I love you, Janet.'

She raised her lips and let him kiss them.

She let herself into her room. She stood a long while gazing out of the window over New York. Once she had thought the only thing in this world she wanted was to marry Mark. She had her opportunity. Surely her love would be strong enough to make him banish all thoughts of Coleen. Until tonight she had thought that all that she really wanted was to have Mark ask her to marry him. Now she was no longer sure of her own feelings. She missed with Mark the close sense of companiship she had with Julian.

She wished she could talk it over with Julian, get his advice on what she ought to do. But mightn't that be a little cruel, to ask his advice when he made no secret of his own love for her?

How long would Mark be content to wait for his answer? She tried to search into her own heart, but she was no longer sure of anything.

The moon was shining brightly into the room. She undressed in a pool of moonlight and crept into bed.

That night she dreamt of Julian. She dreamt he came to tell her that he was going away on a long trip; she might never see him again in this world. She reached out her arms to him. 'Don't go, my darling!' But already he was gone.

When she awoke there were tear-stains on her cheeks. Why should she dream of Julian when last night Mark had asked her to marry him?

# 17

Julian owned a chevrolet convertible. One Sunday he said he would drive her to Newhaven. 'My aunt and uncle live there. They brought me up. Both my parents, as I think I told you, were killed in a car smash when I was a child. I'd like to have you meet them, Janet. My uncle is a doctor; my aunt, my mother's sister, is sweet and good. They are childless, but they are the only family I possess.'

Janet said she would like to meet them and on the Sunday morning they started off for Newhaven. The sun was shining, the skies were blue; the trees on the highways were a vivid green.

'You haven't talked to me much about Mark lately,' he remarked.

Suddenly she felt she wanted to tell him.

'Mark has asked me to marry him.'

His foot pressed down hard upon the accelerator and the car jerked forward. She almost fell against the plate-glass windscreen.

'Sorry,' he said. 'But you do think of things to startle a fellow.'

'I'm sorry I startled you. I was fairly startled myself when Mark put the question to me the other night. Not that we hadn't talked about marriage, but only vaguely.'

'Well, what did you do? Shout hurray and fall into his arms across the dinner table? Did he propose across the dinner table?'

'He did. How did you know, Julian?'

He grinned a little wryly. 'I just guessed. Mark would propose over the dinner table, over coffee and liqueurs. It's in the picture. What did you do, Janet? Did you accept with sufficient gratitude?'

His attitude annoyed her. She had expected sympathetic understanding. But it seemed there were times you could expect too much of a man.

'I didn't accept,' she said. 'I didn't refuse him either.'

'But why didn't you accept? I thought that was the one thing you wanted in this world — to become Mark Dexter's wife. I remember promising you in Honolulu that I'd help you if I could. And now the great chance comes and you don't go all out after it.'

'I hate you when you're sarcastic, Julian.' Her face flushed furiously. 'I'm not sure I really want to marry Mark.'

'How come the change of heart?'

She wondered about that herself.

'I don't think he's ever got over his infatuation for Coleen Hausman,' she said finally.

'You don't think your love is strong enough to make him forget her?'

She hesitated. 'At one time I thought it was. I'm not so sure now.' She added on rather a despairing note, 'I'm no longer sure of anything.'

He half-turned and looked at her. His deep blue eyes were hooded by the prominent brows. 'Poor kid,' he said.

'And just what do you want me to do about it?'

'Why should you do anything about it? I'll have to make up my own mind in time.'

Suddenly she was longing for him to say something more. She was longing for him to say, 'Don't marry Mark. You and I would have a good life together, Janet. We know so much about each other; we understand each other.' But he said nothing. And after all, what she thought was mainly nonsense.

'Do you think if Mark was finally disillusioned about Coleen he would be able to put her entirely out of his thoughts?' he asked abruptly.

She thought about it. 'He might. But what is there to know about Coleen other than what she obviously is — selfish and conceited, but maddeningly attractive?'

'I think there's more to know about her than that,' he said. 'I blame her for Henry's death. I'm convinced she as good as sent him to his death. They might have had a scene and he took too much to drink. No, I don't think that. Henry was too careful when he was driving. I have recently been in touch with the Chinese house-boy they had in Hollywood, Jack Chong. He's in New York with the Van Sittut family. I had a long talk with him the other night. Houseboys hear a lot. Apparently she was continually plaguing Henry to give her a divorce, which he refused. Poor tool, he happened to be very much in love with her. She would urge him to drink, but Jack Chong said he would accept one drink, no more. But on that one night, the night of his death, Jack opened the door to him. He was quite sober; and yet half an hour later when he left the house, he was swaying madly. Jack hesitated, wondering what to do. He ran out into the street, but the car had already started up. When he got back into the kitchen, Coleen was washing out their glasses — a thing she never did. 'I couldn't find you, Jack,' she said, 'so I thought I'd take the glasses out and wash them up.' '

'But nothing of this proves anything,' Janet said. 'And I gather in the court they said the death was accidental.'

'I'd like to follow it up,' Julian went on. 'We may be able to free Mark of his infatuation and then you and he could be married with smiles all round and wedding bells. You'd like that, wouldn't you?'

'Yes,' she said, but her voice was doubtful.

It was a delightful drive through the countryside. Dr. and Mrs. John Leiman's house stood on the corner of a square of old-fashioned houses in Newhaven. Dr. Leiman was a slight, grey-haired man. His wife, Julian's mother's sister, had a far more definite personality. She reminded Janet very much of Julian. She was tall and very lean as Julian was. She had his high cheekbones, his deep-sunken blue eyes. Her hair, now straddled with grey, must have been as dark as his. But she had his same wide welcoming grin.

‘So this is the little girl we’ve been hearing so much about,’ she said.

Janet hadn’t known that Julian had talked to his aunt and uncle about her.

His aunt was very different from Mrs. Dexter. Mrs. Dexter was a sweet, rather faded personality; Julian’s aunt was still strong and vigorous. She expressed herself and her points of view frequently and rather loudly. But Janet liked her. She felt that despite all her mannerisms, she would be a good and a true friend; she would take up a lost cause and fight for it to the death. She had obviously led a harder life than Mark’s mother, who had been reared with every luxury and had married money. This couple, Dr. Leiman and his wife, had had to fight their way to the top of his profession.

‘It’s a tragedy they never had any children,’ Julian said in the few moments they were alone while Mrs Leiman was serving dinner. ‘Aunt Ruth is the matriarchal type. She ought to have had a large family.’

'Did she spoil you very much, Julian?' Janet asked with a smile.

'She bullied me. She both bullied me and spoiled me when I was a kid. But when I started to grow to manhood, she insisted that I stand on my own feet. I went through Yale, then I went to New York looking for a job. But the average job didn't appeal to me. I was too impatient, too restless. I wanted to be out and about amongst people, not sitting cosily in an office.'

'Come along into lunch,' Mrs. Leiman called. 'We've got some fine ribs of roast beef in our guest's honour.'

But as they passed from the sitting-room into the dining-room Janet reminded herself that Julian had never told her just what he did. It seemed strange he hadn't told her. Sometimes he was intensely busy, and other times he seemed to have plenty of free time on his hands. She knew he had had a great deal to do with Tim Warren's jewel-theft activities. She guessed that was why he had warned her not to come to New York in the first place. Now Tim, with the other three men, stood awaiting trial. It was as well, perhaps, that June would never see him behind prison bars.

It was a very agreeable meal. She discovered that Dr. Leiman had a dry sense of humour and Mrs Leiman was obviously in love with him, for she laughed heartily at her husband's jokes. Janet felt very much at home with them. They were more her type of people than the Dexters were, greatly as she had liked them.

'You must bring Janet down for a week-end, Julian,' his aunt said. 'When you have an opportunity to, show her all around the University, the University football bowl and the other attractions of this small city.'

Janet said she'd love to come, and she really meant it.

Just when lunch was finishing, Dr. Leiman received an urgent call. Since his car was in dock over the week-end, he asked Julian to drive him to his case.

Janet helped Mrs. Leiman wash up the dishes.

She gave her that wide cheerful grin as she remarked, 'I never knew that Julian would fall so hard for anyone as he's fallen for you, Janet. Until he met you, he hasn't been much of a one for women. I can't say that I blame him for being in love with you. I only hope you like him, Janet.'

'I like him very much. I . . . ' But she never finished the sentence. She scarcely knew what she had been going to say.

Mrs. Leiman gave her a pat, which was more like a hearty whack between the shoulders. 'Take your time in making up your mind, Janet. In my days marriages were made to last and I still believe they should be.'

'Julian has never told me what he does; he seems to work at such odd hours,' Janet said.

Mrs. Leiman's blue eyes narrowed. 'I think I'd better leave it to him to tell you. But it's not work in any way he need be ashamed of. On the contrary, I think he should be proud. I think you would be proud of him too, Janet.'

They finished the dishes and went back into the lounge. Shortly afterwards Julian and Dr. Leiman returned. They talked a while and then Julian said he must be getting back to New York; he had things to do.

The doctor and his wife stood on the front steps waving to them as they drove away.

'Well, did you like them?' Julian asked.

'I think they're darlings,' Janet returned warmly. 'You are very much like your aunt.'

He grinned at her. 'Then am I a darling too?'

She nodded. 'You're the best friend a girl ever had, Julian,' she said quietly.

# 18

Coleen Hausman was throwing a party. Janet was surprised that she was invited to it. She had never thought that Coleen had any great love for her. When she told Julian about it, he said, 'I think I'll gate-crash that party. I want to have a heart-to-heart talk with Coleen Hausman. A party's as good a time as any. The hostess is usually in a pretty nervous state. She has a drink or two to soothe her nerves. It's a good time to get something out of her if she has anything to tell.'

'You're not afraid she'll ask you to leave?'

He shrugged. 'I'll have to take that risk. This won't be the first party I've gate-crashed. It's all in the nature of my job.'

She leant towards him. 'Just what is

your job, Julian? I do wish you'd tell me.'

'Some day I shall,' he said. 'When you've decided whether or not you are going to marry Mark and whether or not you're going to marry me.'

She saw Mark all the time in the office and occasionally he took her out to lunch or dinner. Several times he asked her if she had reached any decision about his proposal. But she always begged him to give her more time. It was almost as though she was afraid of saying yes. And yet why should she be afraid? But she was no longer certain that she loved him. Was that only because the shadow of Coleen Hausman still hung between them?

The evening of the party was warm and balmy. The moon was half full and there were baskets full of stars. Mark called for Janet. She was wearing her green dinner dress with the tight bodice and bouffant skirt. They met in the foyer.

'You look very lovely tonight, my

dear,' he said. 'Not even Coleen, wearing all her emeralds, could look lovelier.'

'Thank you, Mark.'

'I'd like very much to kiss you,' he said. 'But it's rather public here.'

She laughed. 'You think we'd be giving the reception-clerk ideas?'

Coleen was wearing the famous Cameron Emeralds tonight. This party was by the way of being a celebration for having recovered them. She wore a gown of gold brocade which almost matched her hair. She looked golden and glowing. The only touch of colour was the string of fantastically lovely emeralds around her throat, in her ears, and the heavy emerald bracelet she wore on her arm. Her hair was dressed high and stiffly lacquered in the fashionable manner. The long lines of her figure were perfect.

Janet noticed that Mark couldn't keep his eyes off her. It had been the same way in Honolulu. She had been tortured with jealousy and in complete despair. But now for some reason she wasn't hurt. She couldn't understand it herself, but Mark's obvious infatuation for Coleen was no longer so painful to her.

Coleen's apartment was also a penthouse apartment. There was a wide stretch of garden surrounded by railings. The guests, cocktail glasses in hand, drifted in and out of the apartment on to the patio.

It was fairly late when Julian arrived. For some reason Janet felt her heart beat faster. She was glad that he was there — very glad. She knew unconsciously she had been waiting for him all evening to put in an appearance. She asked herself if she could be in love with Julian. But such a little time ago she had thought it was Mark. Maybe it was still Mark. It was just that the sight of Julian had excited her.

'I didn't know I'd invited you,' Coleen said. Her voice was angry.

Julian shrugged and grinned. 'No, you forgot to send me an invitation, didn't you? But I have to talk to you, Coleen, and it seemed this would be as good a time as any.'

'What do you want to talk to me about?' Her voice was hard and suspicious.

'I think you'll listen to what I have to say,' he said. 'I happened to get in touch with Jack Chong, who was your house-boy in Hollywood.'

She shrugged. 'What of it?'

'He had a little tale to tell, which I think might interest you. It certainly interested *me*.'

A sudden look of fear came into her eyes. 'Can't you talk with me some other time?'

'No, it must be tonight,' Julian said with decision. 'When can we be alone?'

She hesitated. 'The caterers will be serving supper in an hour's time. I'll meet you on the roof garden. We're unlikely to be disturbed there.'

'Very well.'

She left him almost immediately.

Julian finally discovered Janet. For

some reason she felt tired tonight. She was sitting in a secluded corner. He sank down on to a seat beside her, grinning rather wryly. 'Well, how's my girl tonight? Perhaps I shouldn't call you my girl when Mark is present.'

'I don't mind.' She smiled back at him. 'I've been standing talking for an hour. I don't know any of these people and I don't think they're interested in anything I have to say to them. Was Coleen very mad at you for coming?'

'No, I said I wanted to have a little chat with her — not that I think I am at all welcome.' He chuckled grimly.

'I haven't seen you for several days, Julian.'

'Does that mean you've missed me?'

She smiled faintly. 'Yes, I suppose I have. We always seem to have so much to talk about. And you always take me to such fascinating and unusual places in New York.'

'I thought you might be occupied with Mark. Have you reached any decision?'

She shook her head. 'I can't seem to decide.'

'But you were so much in love with him once. It is only because of Coleen Hausman?'

'I don't know,' she whispered. 'I don't honestly know, Julian. Sometimes I think I would like to marry Mark, and at other times he seems almost a stranger to me.'

'Maybe something will happen in the near future which will make it easier for you to decide. Come out on to the patio.'

Mark was still engaged in talking to friends. He seemed to know almost everyone here. She was glad of Julian's company. She had met so many people tonight, heard so many names, her head was in a whirl.

'When are you going to come to Newhaven for that weekend you promised my aunt?' he asked.

She smiled. 'Any time. I like them both so much.'

'I'll see which week-end suits them.

You mean you really want to come?'

She nodded. 'I want to come very much, Julian.'

As they wandered round, Julian put out a hand and touched the railing. It moved as he shook it. 'This railing doesn't look too strong,' he said. 'There's a sheer drop into the street. It might be dangerous.'

'Oh, surely not,' she said.

'I wouldn't know for certain, but it seems to me as though it's badly rusted. Funny how people will go to such pains and expense in interior decoration and omit to notice a thing like this.'

She shivered. 'It would be horrible to drop down between these buildings that are like a cliff-face.'

Inside, Julian met some friends. He introduced Janet, and the four of them talked.

Presently it was time for supper. There was a large dining room in the apartment. All the guests crowded in. Mark rejoined Janet. Julian slipped away and went out into the garden.

Coleen joined him presently.

'Well, what is it you want to say to me?' Her voice was hard; her face was like a mask.

'What I have to say won't take long in telling,' Julian said. 'But maybe you can supply me with a few details. All Henry Hausman's friends know that he didn't drink to excess, although since the motor smash you have been circulating the story that he did. Jack Chong bore me out. He said he had never seen the Master drunk except on one occasion — the night he died. He admitted him. He was quite sober. He went into the lounge and had a drink with you. When he left he was distinctly groggy. Obviously in no condition to drive. What happened in that half-hour, Coleen? Answer me, because I'm determined to have the answer.'

She backed away from him towards the railing. 'There's nothing to tell. Henry had several drinks. We had a row. He said he would go for a spin in the car to cool down. That's all there is to it.'

'Is it?' Julian asked her curtly. 'I don't believe a word you've told me. I think you put something in Henry's drink that night. Why were you so eager to go out into the kitchen and wash the glasses? I think you put a drug in Henry's drink. You as good as murdered him.'

'No!' she cried, and thrust herself farther back against the railing.

Something cracked. She swayed. One of the bars had fallen loose. Julian grabbed her just before she fell. But he didn't immediately pull her back to safety; he merely held on to her.

'Listen, Coleen,' he said. 'I have to know the truth. You're at my mercy now; I've but to let you go and you'll drop down twenty flights. You will be dead by the time you reach the bottom. The bar gave way; it was an accident. Now are you going to tell me the truth? If you do, I'll pull you back to safety. If you don't, I'll let you die. You as good as murdered Henry. No one has seen us out here. Your death will be accidental.'

'No!' she shrieked. 'Pull me back! Pull me back, Julian!'

'What did you put in Henry's drink that night?' His voice thundered at her.

'I . . . ' But she was in too great a state of terror to know what she was saying. 'I just put a few drops in his drink. Nothing much. I didn't mean him to come to any serious harm.'

'You'll tell that same story to Mark?'

'No. Oh, yes, yes! Oh, for heaven's sake, please, please God, pull me back to safety, Julian!'

'Do you promise to tell Mark?'

'Yes,' she gasped.

He jerked her back. The faulty railing crashed into the street below. She was quivering and crying. 'I might be dead! I might be dead,' she kept repeating. 'What are you going to do about it, Julian?'

'Nothing,' he said, 'if you keep your promise and tell Mark. I know I should have you prosecuted, but that won't bring Henry back. But if you don't tell Mark exactly what you told me, I shall most certainly have you prosecuted.'

She looked at him in a scared way. 'Are you a policeman, Julian?'

'I'm connected with the police force,' he told her. 'Now wait there. I'll go in and find Mark.'

She was too overcome with fear, with abject terror, not to do as he told her. She was weeping unrestrainedly. It was from Julian that Mark finally heard the story.

He turned and shook Coleen by the shoulder. 'Is this true?' he demanded.

She shivered. 'I didn't mean to kill him, but I did put some drops in his drink.'

'Oh my God!' Mark said. 'I can't believe it, Coleen.'

'I didn't mean any harm. I swear I didn't mean him any harm,' she kept on sobbing. 'I was just mad at him, that was all. I wanted him to go out into the street and let people think that he was drunk. That would have made it easier for me to get a divorce in Reno. I was sick and tired of Henry. I — I hated him.' She looked pleadingly towards Mark. 'I've never cared for anyone really but you, Mark. I don't know what got into me to make me elope with Henry.'

There was a pause. No one seemed to know quite what to say. Then Mark said, 'You'd better go quickly to your room, Coleen. Wash your face and powder and re-do your make-up. Don't let this party end in a scandal.'

She nodded. She had been crouched on a garden lounge. She groped to her feet.

'Can you get in through the kitchen?' Mark suggested. 'There'll be no one but the kitchen staff there.'

'I'll manage,' she said. But she was trembling so violently when she got up that the men had to help her to the kitchen door. She disappeared inside.

Mark turned towards Julian. 'Why did you do this?'

'I thought it might cure your

infatuation for Coleen. If it has done so, you can explain to Janet and ask her to marry you again.'

'You want me to marry Janet?' Mark almost shouted in astonishment.

'I love her enough to want her to be happy,' Julian said. 'When we were in Honolulu I promised to help her.'

'Then you did it for her sake?' Mark asked.

'I don't know,' Julian said. 'I was also very much attached to Henry Hausman. He was one of my best pals. I wanted to clear his name.'

'You're not going to do anything about it?' Mark asked sharply.

Julian shrugged. 'I didn't do this in the line of duty. I did it off my own bat. I wanted to prove that Coleen had lied about Henry. I also want Janet to be happy. I don't know why, but that's the one thing in this world I do want.'

Janet was surprised at Mark's taut grim face when he came up to her and said that they should leave. She was surprised. Up until the supper break, during which Julian had fetched him outside, he seemed to be enjoying the party very much indeed.

She said, 'I must say good-bye to Julian.'

'Julian has already left,' he told her.

Suddenly she felt inexpressibly hurt. Julian had gone without saying good-bye to her. She too was glad to leave the party. It no longer held any charm or excitement for her.

Mark was grimly silent on his way back to the Beekman Towers Hotel. His attitude was so strange she finally asked tentatively, 'Did anything happen tonight — anything to upset you, Mark?'

'Something happened,' he said, 'but I don't want to talk about it right at this moment, Janet. Do you mind? Perhaps you will dine with me later in the week?'

She nodded. 'If you wish, Mark.'

He left her in the foyer. He didn't even attempt to kiss her good night. He seemed like a man in a trance. Obviously something had happened that night. But what? Would he ever tell her? And why had Julian, having gate-crashed the party so purposefully, suddenly left? Oddly, without even saying good night to her. That seemed the most important thing of all at the moment.

She hesitated for quite a while, but finally she rang his apartment number. His voice answered.

'Why did you leave so suddenly, Julian? You didn't even say good night to me.'

'I thought Mark was looking after you tonight.'

'I know, but all the same . . . we're such good friends, Julian.'

'I hope we shall be — even when you're married to Mark.'

She felt rattled. 'What makes you so sure I'm going to marry Mark?'

'I think you will. I promised to help you in Honolulu, didn't I? I've done so tonight. I think I've cured Mark's infatuation for Coleen for all time. You can go right ahead with the wedding bells.'

'Julian! . . . ' But he had already replaced the receiver.

# 19

She saw nothing of Julian for several days. He didn't telephone her. She kept asking at the reception desk if anyone had called. Every time the phone rang in her office her heart leapt and started to thump madly. But it was never Julian. She hesitated to telephone him after the abrupt way he had put down the receiver on the night of the party. But finally one evening she summoned up her courage and put through a call to his apartment.

The telephone rang for a very long while, but finally he answered it. 'I was in the corridor,' he said, 'when I heard the phone ringing. I came back and answered it. I was on my way out.'

She pocketed her pride. 'You weren't coming to see me, by any chance?'

'No,' he said. 'I have work to do tonight. Are you officially engaged to

Mark yet, Janet?'

'No.'

'What's holding up the celebration? I've done my best — what I promised you I'd do in Honolulu.'

'You're a pig-headed stubborn ass!' And this time it was she who smashed down the receiver.

Mark asked her out to dinner the following night and she agreed to go. He suggested the Village, but the Village was still too painful for her. She had looked in on the Madame June Beauty Salon, but it had already changed hands. A new receptionist was at the desk. She asked for Miss Mary Claire and was told that all the staff were changed now that the salon was under new management.

She felt very sick at heart as she turned away and walked towards Fifth Avenue. June had worked so hard at establishing this business. It had been sold, but where had the money gone? Probably to pay for Tim's defence, or to leave it in the bank as a nest-egg when he finally got out of prison.

Mark and she drove out to Long Island and dined in the open air at a sea food restaurant. There was clam chowder and delicious barbecued lobsters. The moon was full tonight. The whole atmosphere of the small port with its yachts and schooners and motor-launches was most romantic.

'I want to ask you again to marry me,' Mark said as they sat over their coffee. 'I've finally got Coleen right out of my system — at least I hope I have. After what she revealed that awful night, I feel I never want to see her again. She was partially responsible for her husband's death. You knew? I suppose Julian told you.'

'He didn't tell me what happened. He only told me one day when we drove to Newhaven to lunch with his aunt and uncle what he suspected.'

'I'm afraid it was the truth. I think I've known in my heart it was the truth all along. But I didn't want to face it.'

'That was why you asked me to

marry you,' she said. 'To escape?'

'I no longer need to escape. I'm wholly yours, if you want me, Janet.'

She hesitated for quite a while, and then she said, 'I like you so much, Mark. I'm awfully grateful to you as well. At one time I thought I loved you — loved you very much. But I'm sure that if I agreed to marry you now it would be a mistake.'

'You don't love me any more?' His grey eyes probed into hers.

'Not as I should love you to marry you, Mark. I'll finish my six months in your office and then go back to Australia.'

'If Julian Gaden will let you go,' he said. His voice was bitter.

'I haven't seen Julian for over a week.'

'Are you in love with him, Janet?'

'I think perhaps I am,' she said slowly. 'No place is fun when he isn't there. I miss his companionship more than I can tell you. I'm sorry, Mark. You've been so good to me, I'm terribly sorry.'

'If Coleen — damn her — had never met me in Honolulu, we might be married now. She's a witch of a woman, Janet. I know she practically murdered Henry. I blame her bitterly, but I shouldn't want it that we should never meet again.'

She gave him a twisted smile. 'The old attraction still holds, Mark?'

'It's the very devil,' he admitted. 'I keep trying to find excuses for her. It's lucky for her Julian didn't go to the police with the evidence he had uncovered.'

'I think Julian only wanted to set you free.'

'I am free,' Mark said. His lips twisted, his handsome face crumpled. 'It's humiliating that you no longer love me, Janet.'

The romantic scene out on the quay was wasted. They had reached the dead end. Mark paid the bill and they climbed back into the car.

'I can't wish for your happiness with Julian,' Mark said. 'I've never liked the fellow.'

'I didn't like him either in the beginning,' she confessed. 'He's hard and arrogant. But he can be gentle and understanding, too.'

They said good night at the Beekman Towers Hotel almost formally. Mark's pride might be hurt badly, but she didn't believe he had ever been as much in love with her as he had been with Coleen Hausman. Coleen still might win out. A man as infatuated as Mark had been might close his conscience; he might even in time will himself to forget everything that had happened in the past

The desk clerk told her that a Mr. Gaden had been telephoning, would she ring him when she returned to the hotel? Her heart-beat quickened; her cheeks stung with colour. She went up quickly to her room to ring Julian.

'Hello! Is that you, Julian? This is Janet.'

'I've been trying to get in touch with you all evening. I had to leave New York suddenly and fly across to California. It was a matter of urgent business. But I didn't flatter myself you'd miss me. Is the wedding all set?'

'No.'

'How come? Don't say I didn't do my best for you.'

'You did all that was necessary, Julian.'

'Don't tell me you've suffered a change of heart?'

'Maybe I have. Anyhow I'm not going to marry Mark.'

He was silent for several moments and when he spoke again there was a throbbing undercurrent of joy in his voice. 'What I've been ringing for,' he said, 'is that Aunt Ruth wants you to come down to Newhaven next week-end. Can you make it?'

She laughed. 'I'll say I can. I'd love to come.'

'It's two days away. Shall I see you in the meantime?'

'No,' she answered. 'But I'll be ready for you to pick me up on the Saturday morning.'

'I'd like to come round right away,' he said. 'To think I scared that girl almost to death just to wring that confession out of her. I suspected all along what had happened, but I wanted for your sake to have her tell Mark.'

'He may be disillusioned now; he may never marry her; but I think in a way he'll always be in love with her.'

'Some men are fools. Personally, I can't see her attraction. She's conceited and hard-hearted, and it was through her that Henry met his death. I pity Mark if he marries her.'

'I don't know what Mark will do.'

'You're not still as crazy about him as you were?'

'No. Good night, Julian.'

Mark looked at her in a very sad way these days, but he made no comment on her decision not to marry him. But he no longer asked her out to lunch or dinner. She knew she was doing a good job for the firm. Sam Gleeson, the editor, complimented her more than once on her criticism of the various novels, saying what a great help they were to him in making his decisions. But now that Mark and she were no longer so friendly, she didn't suppose he would ask her to stay on after her six months were up. But by her contract she had still three months to go. Had it all happened in the brief space of three months? It seemed incredible.

The two days before Saturday seemed to drag, but it was by her own choice she had kept Julian away from her. She wanted to think out everything very clearly; there must be no mistake this time.

She was wearing a pretty floral dress when he picked her up on the following Saturday in his neat off-white convertible. He looked at her and said softly, 'You look dazzling, honey.'

'I feel pretty good. I'm looking forward to this week-end immensely.'

'Well, I certainly am, too,' he said. 'Somehow when Aunt Ruth first invited you, I never thought it would actually come off. Did you, Janet?'

‘I didn’t know at the time,’ she said. ‘But I liked Dr. and Mrs. Leiman very much — especially your Aunt Ruth. She’s witty and amusing and has great force of character.’

‘You’re saying something there,’ he said, and grinned. ‘Aunt Ruth and I often fight like the devil, but we have great respect for each other.’

They arrived about noon and were welcomed heartily by Julian’s aunt and uncle. She took Janet up and showed her her room. It was large and full of old-fashioned furniture and the carpet was rather threadbare.

She thought in contrast of Mark’s home in Ridgefield, Connecticut. The doctor probably made a decent income, but he wasn’t wealthy. She didn’t think Julian was wealthy either, though he often moved in high society. She was still puzzled about what he did. When would he tell her?

Lunch passed off very pleasantly, after which Julian said he would show her through some of the buildings of

Yale University and the famous Football Bowl.

It was easy to gain admission and walk around, as the students were all on vacation. The big Bowl with its tiers of seats was deserted. She felt so small in comparison with it, they might have been midget figures.

Suddenly they seemed very much alone as though they were the last two people left in this world.

'Why aren't you going to marry Mark?' Julian asked her quietly. 'I think Coleen is out of his life for good. Financially and socially he's a splendid catch. You don't know your onions, girl.' But he grinned down at her with great affection.

'I suppose from a practical point of view I'm being an awful fool,' she agreed. 'I did think I loved Mark once. But lately I've come to realise I didn't. I was infatuated. He is awfully good-looking and very charming.'

'Have you anyone else in mind to marry?' he asked 'Don't answer if I'm speaking out of turn.'

'Yes, I have someone else in mind,' she said. 'He's been in my mind quite a great deal recently. In fact I think he's been in my mind ever since I arrived in New York.'

'You won't tell me his name?'

She knew he was teasing her — or she thought he was.

Suddenly she cried, 'Have I got to ask you to marry me, Julian? Why have you been stubborn for so long? You say you're in love with me, and yet you've never once asked me to be your wife. I could slap your face,' she ended. She was half laughing, half crying.

'My darling, darling Janet.' This time there was something of a sob beneath his laughter. 'You really want to marry me — *me*, when I have so very little to offer you, my pet?'

'I only want to be with you, Julian. That's enough for me.'

'You don't even know what I do to make a living.'

'Does that really matter?'

'It should matter to any sensible girl. But I see you're in no mood to be sensible, my dearest. I'll tell you, although you must keep it as a strict secret. I'm an undercover man working with the New York Police. If the fact became known, I should be useless to the force. As it is, I drift about like a playboy, searching for criminals in all walks of life.'

'You suspected Tim Warren, didn't you? That was why you didn't want me to come over and join my mother? You also knew about Mark and Coleen. I hated you at the time for not wanting me to come, but now I don't hate you any longer.'

'How could you, when I love you so very much? My sweetheart.' He gathered her more urgently into his arms. He kissed her lips, her cheeks, her eyes. 'I think I'm the luckiest person alive. I've quite a decent apartment in the East Seventies, big enough for two. Two — it's a wonderful word, isn't it, when it means just you and me? But you'll be giving up quite a lot by marrying me. I have my salary and, of course, expenses, but I'm far from being a rich man, my darling.'

'I can work,' she told him. 'If not with the East-West Publishing Company, I'll get a job with some other publishing firm.'

'I make enough. You wouldn't have to work.'

'But I want to work for the present. I like my job; I like everything to do with publishing. Of course later, when the children will come, it'll be different. We'll have to move out on to Long Island somewhere.'

'Did you say children?' he asked. 'Oh, my darling, I love you for saying that. I've always longed for a couple of kids of my own. I missed both my parents so much when I was young. I want my kids to have a wonderful family life.'

'We'll give it to them,' she said. 'But that's very much in the future, Julian. Just now I want it to be that magic two — the two of us, my darling.'

They looked into each other's faces. There were suddenly tears in the eyes of both of them.

It was an enchanted place. She nuzzled her head against his shoulder. 'Darling, I'm so happy,' she whispered. 'I never dreamt that I could be so happy in all my life.'

'What do you think I am?' he said, and right there he kissed her once again, full on the lips. 'I know I warned you against coming but, boy, am I glad you came!'

THE END

*Other titles in the*
*Linford Romance Library:*

## SO NEAR TO LOVE

### Gillian Kaye

Despite Emma's dislike of Mr Peirstone, schoolmaster in Ellerdale, she is forced to go to School House to look after his children. There she meets his son, Adam, and falls in love. But Adam's circumstances don't allow for marriage. Then Mr Peirstone dies unexpectedly and Emma goes to work for Dr Redman and his wife, Amy, in Ravendale. The doctor schemes to matchmake Emma and Adam . . . but can there ever be a happy ending for the young couple?

## THE BOYS NEXT DOOR

### Janet Chamberlain

When Ross Anderson and his lively nephews move in next door to Alison Grainger, it ends her well-ordered life — a life that doesn't include children. The noise is bad enough, but Alison becomes critical of Ross's method of childcare even as she becomes attracted to him. She becomes involved in their welfare despite herself. But when it emerges that the boys' grandmother has persuaded Alison to record Ross's progress with the children, the rift between them gets even bigger.

## WHITE LACE

### Rosemary A. Smith

Dismissed from her employment at the academy, the future seems bleak for Barbara Thorpe. But a whirlwind romance leads to marriage when she meets Kieran Alexander. However, upon being taken to his home, Rowan Castle, she is overawed by its grandness. Barbara is further disquieted by the fact that she knows nothing about him, and by meeting the beautiful but arrogant Kerensa Templeton. First her marriage, then her life, will be threatened before she can discover both the truth and real happiness . . .

## CAMPAIGN FOR LOVE

### Ginny Swart

Andrea Ross is an artist in the studio of an advertising agency and for a long time she's been in love with dashing Grant Carter, an accounts executive at a rival company. Then the new art director from America, charming, untidy, critical Luke Sullivan turns her working world upside down — along with her heart. But Luke has demons that haunt him from the past, as well as a string of other women in his life.

## THE PEBBLE BANK

### Sheila Spencer-Smith

Cara Karrivick and her twin sister never knew they had any family on their father's side. But when Cara and Arlene inherit their grandparents' cottage in Polmerrick, Cara visits the house and is delighted when she uncovers so many family secrets. She meets the rather hostile Josh Pellew, but it doesn't spoil her dream of living there. However, as Cara discovers her grandmother's family record, disaster strikes. Can Josh be the one to help her to realise her dream?